# Murder
## in Guanajuato

*A Culinary Mystery*
*by*
*Ruthie Wornall*

# Murder
## in Guanajuato

Ruthie Wornall has cooked up a delectable murder mystery with her novel, "Murder in Guanajuato." What starts out as a dinner party at the Baptist minister's home results in a mysterious murder by poisoning. Rhonda Winters, a teacher and author, finds herself the prime suspect, forced to use her skills as an amateur sleuth to help solve this culinary mystery. Savor the terrific recipes that are sprinkled throughout the book as you try to guess "whodunit."

Guanajuato (pronounced (WA-NA-WA-tō) is the capital of the state of Guanajuato. It is located about 250 miles north of Mexico City, Mexico.

Time: 1998

Place: Guanajuato, Mexico

Characters:

Rhonda Winters- Author, teacher, amateur sleuth.

Rick Winters- Rhonda's husband, retired vice president of a manufacturing company.

Carlos Selva- Architect and friend who designed Rhonda and Rick's home in Guanajuato.

Pedro Martinez- President of insurance firm in Mexico City.

Katie Martinez- Pedro's wife, a tax lawyer.

Reverend Felipe Lopez- Minister of the First Baptist Church of Guanajuato.

Señora Anita Lopez- Minister's wife and math teacher at the University of Guanajuato.

Señora Juanita Rios- Sunday school teacher.

Professor Juan Almire- Retired professor at whose home Rhonda stayed when she attended the University of Guanajuato in 1963.

Professor Claudio Carrillo- Professor of Spanish at the University of Guanajuato.

Doctor Guillermo Selva- Doctor of Internal Medicine. Carlos' uncle.

Ricardo Selva- Carlos' cousin who is an attorney.

Margarita Selva- Ricardo's wife.

Dr. Francisco Gomez- Psychiatrist, Rhonda and Rick's neighbor.

Dr. Marta Gomez- Psychiatrist's wife, a neurologist.

Ted Saxon- Rhonda's paranoid-schizophrenic ex-husband.

Ginger Saxon- Ted's third wife. A psychiatric nurse.

Javier Valdez- Rhonda and Rick's neighbor. Chief of police in Guanajuato.

Nikki Preciosa- Rhonda and Rick's daughter.

Juan Preciosa- Nikki's husband, a homicide detective from San Antonio, Texas.

Camila- Rhonda and Rick's maid.

Jimmy Winters- Rhonda and Rick's son who is a college student at Baylor University in Waco Texas.

Anne Hall- Retired microbiologist.

Derek Hall- Retired executive.

Alejandra- Felipe Lopez' niece.

Elisa- Gomez' maid.

*In Memory of*
*My Mother,*
*Velora Copeland Holt,*
*who made this book possible.*

## Acknowledgment

The House and Courtyard were designed by
Dr. Luis Sosa, professor of Architecture, Mexico City, Mexico

### Note to Readers
*This book is fiction, and the characters and events are fictitious or*
*used fictitiously. The characters have no relation to anyone who has*
*the same name.*

The University of Guanajuato

# Chapter One

Rhonda and Rick Winters had moved into their new mountain top home in Guanajuato, Mexico, only three months ago. They both loved the white stucco Spanish home. It was even more beautiful than the architect, Carlos Selva's designs and blue prints had indicated. The rooms built around an open-air courtyard, were sunny and light, thanks in part to the ornately topped domes above the various sky lights.

After one month of decorating the house in the Mexican style, Rhonda began her new career of teaching English at the University of Guanajuato and Rick began distributing her cookbooks and novels to the bookstores throughout Mexico.

Rick had recently retired after thirty years. He had worked his way up to vice president of a Kansas City manufacturing firm, and Rhonda was a writer.

He and Rhonda had begun building their retirement home over a year ago.

They attended the First Baptist Church of Guanajuato and already had made three good friends: the minister and his wife, Reverend Felipe and Anita Lopez, and their Sunday School teacher, Senora Juanita Rios. Rhonda had also made friends at the university, and they both liked all of their neighbors very much.

One night at dinner Rhonda said, "Rick, this house was made for parties, don't you think? I would love to have a party and invite our new friends and acquaintances. What do you say?"

"That's fine with me. But do you think you have time? Your classes at the University plus the new novel you've just started have been keeping you pretty busy."

"True, but I'd really like to have a party. I want to show off our gorgeous new home! I'm so proud of it."

"Don't you think you ought to wait until we finish the Spanish class we're taking? We need to be able to say more than "Hola. ¿Cómo está usted?"

Rhonda laughed. "I know our Spanish is awful, but most everyone we know can speak some English."

"Some. But not enough that I know what they're talking about," Rick complained.

"We could invite Carlos, Pedro and Katie. They speak excellent English and could interpret for us. I know they live five hours away in Mexico City, but they could drive here together. They would probably like to get away for a weekend."

"That's a good idea," he agreed. "They could spend the weekend with us if they wished."

"We can introduce Carlos as the architect of our mini-hacienda, and he could take the guests on a tour of it if he wants to," Rhonda suggested.

"Sure. That could be a good advertisement for his work. You never know, one of the guests might be interested in building a new house, or else they might recommend him to someone they know."

Rhonda had met Carlos Selva over thirty years ago when they were both twenty one years old and attending the University of Guanajuato. They had remained friends during the years, even though they hadn't seen much of each other until recently. Pedro also was attending the University when Rhonda was there and she had known him nearly as long as she had known Carlos. Though she'd only known Pedro's wife for a year, she liked her very much.

Also, Carlos had introduced Rick and Rhonda to his uncle and cousins and to several of his friends in Guanajuato. He was born here, attended school and the University here, so he still knew many people in town.

"Rick, I want to invite Professor Almire, too," said Rhonda. "He's the guy we visited with last week at the Carrillos' party. Remember, his home was where Rita and I boarded when we were students here mucho years ago!"

"He seemed like a nice gentleman," said Rick, "and he speaks very good English."

"Yes, he does. When Rita and I lived there in his home, he gave two parties for us. I met Carlos at his home at the first party he gave."

"I thought you met Carlos at the University."

"No. At professor Almire's home."

"When shall we have this party?" asked Rick.

"Let's see. Today is February 7th. How about February 28th? That gives us three weeks to send invitations and get ready for it. OK?" asked Rhonda. She thought a minute then said, "I wish our kids could be here. I sure do miss them." Jimmy was in his first year of College at Baylor University in Waco, Texas, and Nikki and her husband, a police detective, lived in San Antonio. "We'll fly to Texas to see them before long," said Rick. "I miss them, too."

About three days before Rhonda's party her friend, their minister's wife, Anita Lopez, phoned her.

"Hi Rhonda," she said, "We're really looking foreward to your party."

"We're looking forward to having you come," replied Rhonda.

She and Anita had "hit it off" the first Sunday she and Rick had attended the Baptist Church. Not only was Anita the minister's wife and also in their Sunday school class, but she spoke perfect English and they were both teaching classes at the University. They were about the same age and they had a

9

lot in common.

"I have a favor to ask," Anita said. "You know I told you that I attended college in the United States many long years ago?"

"Yes," Rhonda answered tentatively, wondering what the favor was.

"My college roommate phoned me today and told me she was bringing her new husband to Guanajuato for a vacation and asked if they could stay with us. They will arrive tomorrow. Would you mind if I bring them to your party?"

"Please bring them," Rhonda said. "No problem at all."

However, as it turned out, Anita's guests were a problem. A big problem.

# Chapter Two

Rhonda decided to prepare the food for the party herself, since she wanted to serve American food. As the author of a dozen fast and easy cookbooks, the food preparation was not difficult. During the past week she had baked desserts, cookies, brownies and appetizers, then had frozen them.

Today she was making sausage balls, mixing together two cups of Bisquick baking mix, one cup shredded Cheddar cheese and one pound of hot spiced bulk sausage. The mixture was so thick it was hard to mix with the wooden spoon she was using. She put it aside and began mixing it with her hands.

She wondered if she ought to double the recipe. These sausage balls were delicious, she thought as she shaped the mixture into small balls and placed them in a large pan to be baked for twenty minutes at 350 degrees F. Just as she decided to mix up a second batch, the doorbell rang. She washed her hands quickly and went to the door. It was her maid, Camila.

"Buenos Días, Senora Winters," she said, smiling.

"Buenos Días, Camila. I'm so glad you are here. Do you mind polishing silver before you start cleaning?" she asked in her halting Spanish.

Camila knew one word of English so far, and she used it. "OK" she said, then went into the kitchen to find the silver polish and some clean dish towels.

While the sausage balls were baking, Rhonda sat down at the round table in the breakfast nook and checked the party menu and the list of "things to do."

She needed to go to the grocery store. She wished Rick were here to go for her, but he had driven to Leon and Irapuato this morning to distribute her books to several bookstores and gift shops and to also call on new accounts while there. Since they only had one car in Guanajuato, she phoned a taxi. She didn't like to drive through the narrow, winding streets and the subterranean tunnels. She was afraid she might hit another car in such narrow spaces. Also the constant honking made her nervous.

She found her purse, applied lipstick, then told Camila where she was going. She walked down the circular staircase to the front door where she waited for the taxi.

At the grocery store she wheeled her cart to the meat counter and asked the butcher to choose a lean ten pound pre-baked ham. As she stood looking at the other meats while he wrapped the ham, a tall, thin man approached her.

"My lands!" he exclaimed. "Is this a small world or what?"

She looked at him, puzzled, then realized that he looked vaguely familiar.

"What are you doing here, Rhonda?" he asked.

She stared at him a moment, then asked, "Are you Ted?"

"Sure," he grinned. "See, a bad penny always returns!"

"Bad is the definitive word there," she said dryly.

"Oh, Rhonda, be nice to me," he said. "I haven't seen you in so long."

"Where's your wife? Melanie or Meredith or whatever her name is."

"Marion died about ten years ago."

"Oh no! What happened?" she asked. "Did you stick your .357 magnum at her head and squeeze the trigger?"

"You're sure getting negative in your old age," he said dryly.

"In MY old age! I'm not the one standing here with gray hair and wrinkles," she replied irritably.

"If it weren't for hair dye and face lifts you would be."

"Thank you, sir, for the compliment, but my hair isn't dyed

and my face hasn't been lifted. But back to your problem. What happened to Marion?"

"She was shot," he replied, "but the police have not yet apprehended her murderer."

Fear raced through Rhonda's veins. Knowing Ted, her ex-husband as she did, she suspected he was the murderer that the police had not yet apprehended. She remembered only too well the times he had beaten her and pointed his gun at her head. She felt lucky to have gotten out of that marriage alive. She decided she had better not say anything to anger him.

"Ted, I'm so sorry to hear about Marion. Have you remarried?"

"Yes, Ginger and I were married a year ago yesterday. We are here on a delayed honeymoon to celebrate our first anniversary."

Rhonda thought to herself that Ginger must have money and must have paid for the trip. She couldn't remember Ted ever paying for anything. He gambled away his paychecks before he ever got home with them.

"That's nice," she said aloud. "I hope you two enjoy yourselves, and that the third time is the charm for you!"

"Thanks. Are you still married?"

"Certainly."

"Then why don't you and I call a truce, and let's all go out for dinner one night soon?"

"We'll see about that, Ted. I hope you'll do me a favor and not tell anyone in Guanajuato that you and I were formerly married."

"Whatever you say, Senora," he agreed. But Rhonda knew he couldn't be trusted.

"I have to go now," she said as she began to wheel the cart to the next aisle. "Good luck and adiós!"

He caught up with her. "Why are you buying groceries? Do you live here? I remember you attended the University of

Guanajuato the summer before I met you."

She didn't want him to know that she owned a home here or that she was living here. "I'm in a hurry, Ted. I have to go. So long!" she said, ignoring his question, then turned the cart toward the check out stand.

He followed her. "Can I carry your groceries for you, Bubbles?" he asked, using his old pet name for her.

"No thanks, Ted. I have a taxi waiting. The driver will do that for me." She walked away and got into the shortest line.

When she returned home, she kept thinking about Ted. She hoped she would never see him again. Knowing he was in the same town with her put a cloud over her former happy mood. She took her black poodle, Cleopatra, for a walk, then returned home and made a batch of Dishpan cookies, her mother's favorite cookie recipe, then froze them for the party.

Rick arrived in time to eat dinner with her. As they were having dessert she said, "You would never guess in a hundred years who I saw at the grocery store today."

"Your brother?" he guessed.

"No. More remote than that. I saw Ted Saxon, my paranoid ex-husband."

"Is the Mafia still after him?" Rick asked, laughing, referring to the many times Ted had told Rhonda that the Mafia was out to get him. To hear Ted tell it, they watched his apartment, his place of work, and even stationed someone in front of the church they attended on Sundays to keep an eye on him.

"This isn't funny, Rick," admonished Rhonda. "He's just ruined my day. I'm so afraid he will find out where I live."

"So what? He knew you lived in Kansas City the past thirty some odd years, and he never bothered you. Stop worrying about him."

"I don't know why, Rick," she said, "but I have a really bad feeling about him being here."

# Chapter Three

Finally the evening of the party arrived. Camila had cleaned every nook and cranny and also had the silver and crystal sparkling. She had even offered to stay and help Rhonda set up the tables in the courtyard, arrange and serve the food, then clean up after it was over.

Camila sliced the ham and made sandwiches while Rhonda arranged bowls of her homemade mustard, mayonnaise and horseradish beside them. Next, she brought out the trays of fresh vegetables with an onion dip and fresh fruit with a marshmallow cream cheese dip. She arranged platters of Tuna Ball and crackers, sausage balls, cheese balls, a pot of chili con queso with Fritos, and several other appetizers then she brought out her favorite foods: cookies, brownies, coconut balls, chocolate fudge and hello Dollies. Nuts and mints rounded out the buffet. She was serving only tea, coffee, coca cola and a fruit punch to drink. She knew some of the guest would be disappointed that there were no mixed drinks.

Just as she had finished arranging the food and drinks, the doorbell rang. She was happy to see that her first guests were Carlos, Pedro and Katie. They all hugged her and shook hands with Rick. "You look pretty tonight, Rhonda," Carlos said, smiling.

"I love your house," Katie said. She had been here once before, but Rhonda had made several improvements since she had first seen it.

"Thanks," Rhonda smiled. "I'll show you where the food is. Come and have a bite of something."

Katie picked up a tiny sandwich and took a bite. "Umm...this is good. How did you prepare the ham?"

"It's very easy. I just bought a pre-cooked ham, scored it and studded it with whole cloves, placed it in a pot and poured two cups of Coca Cola over it."

"Did you cook it covered?" Katie wanted to know.

"Yes, I covered it with a lid and baked it for two hours at 325 degrees F. Oh, and I basted it a couple of times during the last thirty minutes of baking time with more cola."

"Delicious," Katie murmured between bites. "What does the coke do for it? Give it a good flavor?"

"Yes, that and also it tenderizes it."

Pedro asked, "Where is the booze?"

"Now, Pedro," laughed Rhonda, "You know Baptists are tee-totalers! Have some punch."

"Remember the sculpture of five early civilizations that I promised to give you as a house-warming gift?" asked Carlos. "I have it in the car. Shall I get it and hang it for you before everyone gets here?"

"Sure," said Rhonda. "I can't wait to see it.

"Do you need me to help carry it in?" Rick asked.

"No, it's not that heavy," said Carlos, "but get a hammer for me, will you?"

After the sculpture was hanging and duly admired Rhonda said, "I've got something to tell you three. You're the only people in Mexico who know that I had been previously married to a woman-beating paranoid, named Ted Saxon and I hope you won't tell anyone else."

"Of course not," said Carlos.

"You won't believe what a small world it is! I haven't seen him since 1965, and he showed up at the grocery store yesterday when I was buying the ham!"

"Oh no!" said Katie.

"Hopefully he has left by now," Rhonda said.

Carlos grinned and said, "You've always liked triangles, Rhonda."

The door bell rang. Rhonda excused herself and went to the door. When she opened it, she suddenly felt sick to her stomach.

# Chapter Four

"Rhonda, aren't you going to invite us in?" asked Reverend Felipe. "I want you to meet our guests."

Not waiting for the introductions, Ted asked, "Hi, Rhonda, I'll bet you weren't expecting to see me so soon, were you?"

"No, I wasn't," she said, managing a smile. She glanced at the attractive blonde woman with him and asked, "Aren't you going to introduce us?"

"This is my wife, Ginger."

"Hi Ginger. I'm happy to meet you. Mucho gusto," she smiled. "Hello Felipe and Anita. Come in. I guess you didn't know that Ted and I knew each other many long years ago when he lived in Kansas City? Seeing him again was certainly a surprise."

"Well, isn't it wonderful to get to see an old friend?" enthused Felipe.

Rhonda thought to herself that no it was not wonderful, but she put on the face of a party hostess and said, "I want to introduce you to my other guests. Come on out to the courtyard."

They followed her out and she made the introductions. Everyone chatted a few minutes then Anita said, "Isn't it interesting that Rhonda and Ted know each other?"

Rick, Carlos, Pedro and Katie all turned their head at the same time and looked at her questioningly.

"Ironical, isn't it?" she asked, smiling her hostess smile. "I met both Carlos and Ted the same year. And here we are all together!"

She was saved from further comment when the doorbell rang again.

After that many others arrived and she and Rick stayed busy greeting their guests and introducing them to those they didn't know or in leading them to the tables laden with food and beverage in the courtyard. The evening was warm and many sat or stood in the open air courtyard chatting and snacking.

When everyone had arrived Rhonda introduced Carlos to the group as the architect who had designed and supervised the construction of this home.

"It's beautiful, Carlos," complimented Juanita Ríos, who was Rhonda and Rick's Sunday School teacher.

"Could we go on a tour of your house?" asked Margarita, who was Carlos' cousin.

"Certainly," said Rhonda, "and I'll bet Carlos would do the honors of taking anyone who wants to go on the grand tour."

"Of course," Carlos agreed. "I'll be happy to."

Rhonda's favorite color was red, so she didn't have to decorate too much for her party. The house already looked bright and cheerful.

Carlos began the tour at the front door, then led them up the circular staircase to the foyer. The living room was to the left, the dining room to the right and the courtyard straight ahead. The bedrooms were on the left side of the house and the kitchen, breakfast nook and garage were to the right. The rooms surrounded the courtyard. His tour then returned to the circular staircase and went on upstairs to the round tower office. Guests walked onto the roof or stepped onto the balcony over-looking the street. Everyone seemed to think the house was creative and imaginative which caused Carlos to beam with pride.

Soon Ted cornered Rhonda and made a point to talk privately with her. "Well, Bubbles, you have come up in the world since I last saw you."

"God has been good to us," she replied, piously.

"We'll have to get together soon. Possibly the Lopez' will invite you and Rick to dinner," he suggested.

"Maybe they will," she replied, inching away from him.

When Rick saw she was cornered, he came to the rescue. "Well, Ted, I've heard a lot about you. What are you doing now?"

"I'm currently out of work and Ginger is on vacation, so we decided this was a perfect time to come to Mexico," he replied.

Ted was generally always out of work, Rhonda thought to herself. She remembered he had had four different jobs during their first year of marriage. "Poor Ginger," she thought.

"Where does Ginger work?" Rhonda asked.

"She's a nurse," he replied proudly. "An RN."

"Really? What type of nursing does she do?"

"Psychiatric Nursing."

"No joke? Where did you meet her?" Rhonda asked, pointedly. She suspicioned he had met her when he was a patient in the psychiatric ward of a mental hospital.

Instead of answering her question he said, "There's Ginger. I think she's looking for me. Excuse me."

After Ted had walked away Rhonda said, "Thanks Rick for rescuing me."

A few minutes later she saw Ted and Ginger arguing. It looked like she was trying to calm him down. Then Rhonda saw Ted grab Ginger's arm and practically drag her down the hall out of view. Rhonda followed and when she caught sight of them she called, "Ginger, can you come here a minute? I want to introduce you to someone."

Ted turned her loose and she scurried to Rhonda's side. "Thank you," she said, trembling.

Rhonda pretended she hadn't noticed the trembling and steered her to her neighbor, who was a psychiatrist, and introduced them. "I wanted you to meet Ginger because you two have something in common. You're a psychiatrist and she is a psychiatric nurse."

They shook hands and he asked her where she had worked, then Dr. Gomez's wife, Dr. Marta Gomez, joined them and was introduced to Ginger.

Rhonda told them that Ginger and Anita Lopez had been college roommates in the States and that she and her husband were guests of the Lopez family.

Knowing that Ginger would be temporarily safe from her abusive husband as long as she was in the company of the two doctors, Rhonda excused herself and made the rounds, visiting with each of her other guests. She made it a point to speak to professor Almire. "I want you to know what a wonderful time I had when my roommate Rita, and I lived in your home that summer in Guanajuato and how much we appreciated the parties you gave for us."

She joined Ricardo and his wife, Margarita Selva, Carlos' cousins whom she had met the previous summer. I'm so glad you two could come," she said, smiling. "Have you had enough to eat? There's plenty more. Let's don't let it go to waste!"

Just then Ricardo's dad, Dr. Guillermo Selva, joined them. "Lovely party, Rhonda," he said.

"Thank you," she replied, smiling. "Did all of you go on a tour of the house with Carlos?"

"We did. Carlos outdid himself, didn't he?" asked Ricardo.

"It is thanks to Ricardo and Margarita that we have this land. They found it for us," she said to Guillermo.

You certainly have a great view of the mountains on every side of your house," he said.

Before she could answer. Ted barged in on the conversation and said abruptly, "I have to talk to you, Rhonda."

Rhonda excused herself and walked to an isolated corner

with him. "That was rude of you to drag my wife off to meet someone when I was talking to her," he began.

"Then I do apologize, Ted," she said sarcastically.

"That's OK," he said, his mood changing. Then in an attempt at humor he said, "In our marriage I'm the flash and she's the cash!"

Rhonda couldn't resist retorting, "I knew you wouldn't be the cash since you can't hang onto it. Are you still gambling?"

"I'm going to ignore that this time because what I wanted to talk to you about is that man standing there by the fireplace. Do you know him? Ted asked, pointing to a slim middle aged man.

"Sure, I know him. He's my neighbor."

"He's going to be your black and blue neighbor if he doesn't stop staring at my wife. I don't like it."

"Oh Ted. Don't try to pick a fight. I don't think he's staring at her."

"He certainly is. I've been watching him."

"Why don't you try to think about something pleasant and just ignore him. Remember the expression, 'It's OK to look if you don't touch'."

"How can I think of something pleasant when he keeps staring at her?" he complained. "I'm going over there and teach him a lesson!"

"I wouldn't do that if I were you, Ted. You don't know who you are dealing with there," she warned, then she put her hand on his arm and said, "Let's go to the courtyard and get some punch."

He angrily brushed her hand off his arm and ignoring her advice, he stomped across the room to the man's side. Knowing the man's identity, Rhonda was amused. When she moved closer to them in order to overhear their conversation, she heard Ted say, "Keep your eyes off my wife!"

"Who's your wife?" the man inquired, quietly.

"The woman you've been staring at, that's who! I've been watching you, and if you know what's good for you, you'll get out of here right now!" Ted's voice was getting louder with each sentence and Rhonda noticed that the room had gotten quiet and the guests were also listening to his conversation.

"I'm not going anywhere," retorted her neighbor. "You are the one who had better leave. Who are you, anyway?"

"Let's go outside and fight this out like men!" shouted Ted.

Carlos walked over to Rhonda and asked, "What is going on?"

"Ted is going haywire. He has the delusion that Javier has been staring at his wife and he wants to fight him!" Rhonda answered, grinning.

Carlos laughed, "The entertainment is about to start!"

Just then the neighbor that Ted was harassing flashed his badge and said "Allow me to introduce myself. I am Javier Valdez, Comandante or Chief of Police of Guanajuato. Now Señor you can either leave quietly or I will personally escort you to jail for disturbing the peace. You know what they say about Mexican jails, that once you are in it's hard to get out. The bulge in my jacket is my revolver, so don't cause me to have to use it."

The guests had gathered in the living room and foyer and were listening to the two men. One of those watching the exchange was the Reverend Felipe Lopez. He walked to Ted, took his arm and said calmly, "Let's go home now, son." Then they walked out of the room together, their wives following.

After they were gone, Rhonda walked over to the Comandante and said, "Javier, I'm so sorry that happened. Confidentially, I think that man has a mental problem and he doesn't have much common sense or self-control. I hope you will understand, over-look it and accept my apologies."

He took Rhonda's hand and patted it, "It's forgotten," he said.

She smiled at him and said, "You're very kind. Muy amable!"

Rick came over and said, "I guess I missed the excitement."

She rolled her eyes toward the ceiling as they walked away together and said, "This was an example of what I had to put up with when I was married to him."

Carlos, who also had seen the diversion, joined them and said, "Well, Rick and Rhonda, your party got lively didn't it?"

"Ted chose the perfect person to pick on," Rhonda laughed, her eyes sparking with amusement.

Carlos shook his head, "It's amazing how people from your past keep turning up!"

She grinned, "I was happy you turned up, but I hope that's the last I see of Ted!"

Side street in downtown Guanajuato

# Party Menu

### Coca-Cola Ham

1 (10 to 12 pound) cooked
   boneless ham

2 cups Coca Cola
Whole cloves

Score a cooked boneless ham. Stud with whole cloves. Place ham in a roaster. Pour 1 cup Cola over it. Cover tightly with lid or foil. Bake 2 hours at 325 degrees F. During the last 30 minutes of baking, baste occasionally with the second cup of Cola. Serves 20. Serve on tiny biscuits, mini croissants or small rolls.

### Ann's Mustard

1 cup white vinegar
1 cup sugar

2 ounces Coleman's dry
   mustard
2 eggs

Mix together vinegar and dry mustard and let stand over night. The next day add sugar and eggs and cook until boiling. Boil for five minutes. Let cool, cover and then refrigerate.

### Sausage Balls

2 cups Bisquick baking mix
1 pound hot sausage

1 cup shredded Cheddar
   cheese

Mix the three ingredients together with wooden spoon or your hands. Shape into balls. Place on jelly roll pan and bake at 350 degrees F. for 20 minutes. Drain on paper towels. These freeze well. Makes about 3 dozen small balls. Serve on wooden picks.

## Tuna Ball

1 (8 ounce) package cream
    cheese, softened
1/2 package Lipton dry onion
    soup mix

1 (6 1/4 ounce) can white
    tuna, drained

Combine ingredients; mix well. Shape into a ball. Chill 4 to 6 hours. Serve with crackers, chips, or raw vegetables. Serves 8.


## Cream Cheese and Beef Ball

1 (8 ounce) package cream
    cheese, softened
1 bunch green onions, chopped

3 packages chipped beef,
    chopped fine

Combine cream cheese, 2 packages chipped beef and onions and mix well. Shape into a ball. Refrigerate. Roll the cheese ball in the additional package of chopped beef.


## Chili Con Queso

1 pound Velveeta cheese
1 ( 10 oz) can Ro-Tel
    tomatoes, drained

1 to 2 chopped green
    onions or chives

Melt Velveeta cheese in top of double boiler. Stir in 1 can drained Ro-Tel tomatoes. Heat and stir until hot. Sprinkle chopped green onions or chives over top. Serve with Fritos or tortilla chips. Serves 8-12.

## Fresh Fruit Dip

1 (8 ounce) package cream
   cheese, softened
1/2 teaspoon vanilla

1 (7 oz) jar marshmallow
   creme

Combine and mix well. Serve as a dip surrounded by fresh fruits (strawberries, cantaloupe, banana slices, etc.). Makes 2 cups.

## Red Cabbage Basket of Dip

Red cabbage
1 package Lipton's dry onion
   soup mix

1 (12 ounces) carton sour
   cream

Combine dry onion soup mix with sour cream. Mix the dip well. Cut top off of a washed red cabbage. Hollow out to form a basket or cup. Fill with onion dip. Place in center of platter and surround it with fresh vegetables: Carrot sticks, celery, olives, zucchini sticks, etc. Or serve with potato chips, if preferred.

## Mother's Dishpan Cookies

2 cups brown sugar
2 cups white sugar
2 teaspoons vanilla
2 cups oil
4 eggs
1 cup chopped nuts
4 cups flour

2 teaspoons soda
1 teaspoon salt
1 1/2 cups quick oats
4 cups corn flakes
1/2 cup raisins
1/2 cup coconut
1/2 cup chocolate chips

Cream the first 5 ingredients together. Add flour, soda and salt. Fold in oats, then corn flakes, chocolate chips, coconut, raisins and nuts. Drop onto cookie sheet and bake 7-8 minutes or until brown at 350 degrees F. (Makes a dishpan full!) We add 1/2 cup wheat germ and 1 cup dried cranberries to these cookies (optional).

## Brickle Chip Brownies

1 box brownie mix
1 package brickle chips

1/2 cup chopped pecans

Prepare brownie mix according to package directions. Stir in brickle chips and pecans. Bake as package directs. Serves 8 to 10.

## Hello Dolly

1 stick butter
1 cup chocolate chips
1 cup pecan halves

1 cup graham cracker
  crumbs
1 cup shredded coconut
1 can Eagle Brand milk

Melt butter in bottom of a 9x9 inch pan. Press graham cracker crumbs in bottom of pan. Layer remaining ingredients. Bake at 350 degrees for 30 minutes. Cool and cut into squares and serve.

## Coconut Balls

1 (7 ounce) package shredded
  coconut
1 teaspoon vanilla

2/3 cup Eagle Brand
  sweet condensed milk

Combine the 3 ingredients and mix well. Shape into balls. Bake on greased cookie sheets for 15 minutes at 350 degrees F. Yield: 3 dozen.

# Chapter Five

The next afternoon after church, Ginger phoned Rhonda. She was very apologetic. "Apparently Ted didn't take his medication," she said.

"What kind of medicine does he take?" Rhonda asked.

"He's paranoid-schizophrenic," Ginger explained, "and his symptoms start coming back when he doesn't take his medicine as prescribed. Schizophrenia is a biological disease of the brain. It is treatable, but there is no cure."

"Then why wouldn't he take the pills?" Rhonda wondered.

"Because of the severe side effects that bother him. Also, sometimes his voices tell him not to take the medicine. They often tell him it's poison. You saw what he is like when he misses a dose. He's easily slighted, argumentative and quick to take offense. He sees plots where none exist."

"Don't worry about it Ginger. At least he put a little LIFE into the party!" she joked.

"Do you know anything about this disease?" Ginger asked.

"Not much, but I did take an Abnormal Psychology class when I was in graduate school. I remember about the hallucinations and delusions. I didn't know what was wrong with Ted back when I knew him. I thought he might be paranoid. He was always looking out the window to see if anyone was stationed outside spying on him. Also he was abusive. I thought perhaps he was just born mean."

"He has a terrible, terrible disease," she said. "I should have known better than to have come on this trip. The day before we left, he told me something was going wrong in his head. He seems to be aware of the malfunctioning of his brain.

His thinking that Senor Valdez was staring at me is an example of his delusional thinking. He also has auditory hallucinations in which voices tell him, even command him to do certain things, which may have been what happened last night."

"Can't the doctor change his medication to one without the side effects?" Rhonda asked.

"He has tried several different pills but the one that he is on now controls the voices best--if he takes it. He has a pill to take to control the side effects, but he often forgets to take it."

"I'm very sorry for both of you. It must be terrible," Rhonda said.

"Believe me, it is!" agreed Ginger. "Before his birthday I asked what gift he wanted, and he said, 'A mind!' He said some days it feels like having a blender in his brain mixing things up, and other times the voices shout at him, cursing him and belittling him. Sometimes he sits with his hands clasped tightly over his ears, or else he puts ear plugs in his ears, hoping that will keep him from hearing them."

"Oh Ginger! I had no idea it was this bad. He never explained any of that to me. How very sad."

"Sometimes he says life is like being in the Twilight Zone. He tries to joke about it and says, "Oh, how I miss my mind!" No wonder he gets depressed. He needs patience and understanding," she said, "and that's what I try to give him. I'm going to dedicate my life to caring for him."

"That's admirable, Ginger. He's very lucky to have you. I imagine most people are like me and have neither the patience nor the understanding to deal with such a problem. But aren't you afraid of him? Don't you think he's dangerous? I know he can be violent!"

"Not when he takes his medicine," she said, defending him.

"Yet we know he does not always take it. I hope you will

be very careful," Rhonda said, then asked, "By the way, how did you meet him?"

"I was his nurse during his last hospitalization," she said, confirming Rhonda's earlier supposition.

"You met him in a mental hospital? You knew he was paranoid-schizophrenic, that he was dangerous, yet you still married him?" Rhonda asked. "Why? You're a well-educated woman, and you should have known better."

"Who would take care of him if I didn't? He had no one. His wife and his grandmother who had taken care of him had died. He had almost no friends. I married him because he needed me, and also because I love him."

"I'm happy that he has you, but please be careful. Take care of yourself."

"I will. He told me he used to date you, but I have a suspicion that you were his first wife. I know Marion was his second wife and that his first one lived in Kansas City."

"You are right, but I hope you won't tell it. I would prefer that people don't know. I had asked him not to tell anyone, but I wondered if he hadn't told you?"

"No, he hadn't told me," she said.

"Unlike you, I had no idea he was mentally ill. Had I known I would never have let him inside my door!"

The statue of Pípila stands at the top of the hill overlooking the
Main Plaza, El Jardín de la Union, in downtown Guanajuato.

# Chapter Six

On Sunday evening Dr. Francisco Gomez, the psychiatrist, who lived next door, phoned Rick and Rhonda to thank them for a lovely party.

"I'm so glad you enjoyed it," said Rhonda. "I'm sorry about the argument that erupted before it was over, though."

"That wasn't your fault. Sometimes those things can't be helped," he said. "The guy really has a problem, doesn't he?"

"A big problem," Rhonda agreed.

"I wonder if he is on medication?" the doctor inquired.

"It didn't take you long to figure out what was wrong," she said.

"I noticed the earlier episode with his wife. That was wise of you to rescue her the way you did," he said, complimenting her.

"Can I tell you in confidence what his wife said is wrong with him?"

"Certainly," he said. "It won't go any further."

"His wife said he is paranoid-schizophrenic," Rhonda confided. "I guess he can't help himself, can't control his actions."

"Most schizophrenics do have some control and they can be held partially responsible for their behavior," the doctor replied.

"I talked to his wife. She said he had been hospitalized last year and that he had been on medication. Apparently he either quit taking it or he had just missed a dose before he came over here. She said he had quite a problem with side effects, but he did have a pill to counteract them, though he didn't always remember to take it."

"She should make sure he takes it every day without fail. I'd like to talk to her about it. Perhaps that can be arranged at a later date," he said and added, "My concern is that he may be dangerous, Rhonda. Be very careful. Stay away from him."

"I intend to, believe me! I'm sure he can be violent."

"I wonder if the Lopez family is aware of his illness?" he asked.

"I doubt it," Rhonda said. "I'm sure Ted wouldn't want it told. He would be afraid they might ask them to leave."

"They ought to be told, but Ginger would be the one to tell them. You don't want to get mixed up in that situation in any way, or do anything which might make him angry. Taking care of a person with schizophrenia may be compared to a man who rolled a huge stone uphill only to have it roll back down again, then repeating the exercise over and over again every day."

"Ginger told me a little about the disease. It is terrible," Rhonda said.

"Yes, it is. She may need help with him. Please give her my phone number and tell her to phone me night or day, if she needs me."

"Francisco, you are a very nice man," Rhonda complimented," and I know she will appreciate your offer very much."

"Thank you," he replied. "One more thing before I go. I have an informative book about paranoid-schizophrenia which I will loan you, if you and Rick are interested in reading about it. I am on my way out the door right now. I can drop it by if you want it."

"Yes, we'd love to borrow it," said Rhonda.

"I'll be right over. Good to talk to you. Goodbye."

Rhonda sat up late that night reading the book, and for the first time she felt that she now somewhat understood the reasons why Ted had acted as he did.

# Chapter Seven

Rhonda took a taxi to the University of Guanajuato on Monday morning because Rick needed the car to distribute books in San Miguel de Allende. She taught two English classes there at the University on Mondays, Wednesdays and Fridays. Since she didn't speak fluent Spanish her English classes were conducted almost entirely in English, which actually was better for the students. Whenever they began to ask questions in Spanish she would say, "No hablo Espanol." (I don't speak Spanish), then they had to re-phrase their questions in English, which was good practice for them. She liked her students very much. She had always enjoyed teaching, but it had been eighteen years since she had taught school in the States.

Rhonda had asked her friend, the Spanish professor at the University, Dr. Claudio Carrillo, to come to her English class and make an announcement in Spanish inviting her two classes to a luncheon at her house on Wednesday after class. She needed an interpreter for the invitations so there would be no misunderstanding about the date and time. After Dr. Carrillo made the announcement, Rhonda passed out written invitations with her address and a map of how to get to her home. The students all seemed pleased about the invitation and nearly everyone said they would be able to come.

Having her students for lunch was Rhonda's method of both providing a pleasant outing for them and also a way of getting rid of her leftovers which she had frozen. She had plenty of ham and rolls left and knowing that the leftover appetizers, fudge, brownies and cookies would be too much of a temptation for her, she decided to disperse of them in this manner. She had been on a diet and did not want to gain back the weight she had lost.

After her classes were over she took the bus home and made some vegetable soup for lunch, then she took her poodle, Cleopatra, for a walk. When she returned home she kicked off her shoes and phoned Ginger.

"Hi Ginger!" she greeted her. "I wondered if you would like to come here for lunch on Wednesday around 1:00?"

"I'd love to!" Ginger replied.

"Great! I've invited both of my English classes so they will eat up my leftovers from Saturday night's party. All I have to do is defrost, heat and assemble, and Camila will be here to serve and clean up. I thought perhaps we could talk after the kids are gone."

"I'll be there," promised Ginger, "and if there's anything I can do to help, you just let me know."

After class on Wednesday the students and Ginger arrived. They were very complimentary about the house, the decor and the 360 degree panoramic view of the mountains.

Rhonda had certainly known how to get rid of her leftovers. Her students had dived into the food, eaten to their heart's content, and emptied every platter. She had given them xerox copies of all the recipes in case they wanted to prepare them in their own homes.

After the students had gone, Rhonda invited Ginger to join her in her round tower room office. Ginger walked onto the balcony of the tower room and exclaimed, "What a gorgeous view you have! Do you know that you can even see the El Cristo Rey statue of our Lord on top of Cubilete Mountain from here? Felipe mentioned last night that it is located twenty six miles away. They are taking us to see it tomorrow."

When Ginger came back inside, Rhonda went to her desk and took a slip of paper lying on top of it and handed it to her.

"This is Dr. Francisco Gomez' phone number. He phoned me on Sunday and expressed concern for you. He wanted me to give you this phone number and tell you that you could call him anytime during the night or day if you had a problem and needed to talk. He also said he would be happy to talk with Ted or see him professionally."

"Thanks. That was nice of him," Ginger said, putting the phone number in her pocket.

They sat down on the couch and Ginger said, "Confidentially, I brought Ted to Mexico because he is continuing to think that the Mafia is spying on him and that they are out to get him. That, of course, is a paranoid delusion. However, the delusion is very real to him. I told him the Mafia would never find him in Guanajuato, Mexico, in the home of a Mexican minister and his wife."

"Ginger, he thought the Mafia was after him thirty five years ago when I knew him in Kansas City. He used to hide behind drapes and peer out the window, scanning the area for a person who was spying on him. He told me he had given evidence against the Mafia in a Grand Jury, and that he hoped to get into a Witness Protection Program before they killed him."

"At least his delusions are consistent," Ginger said, rolling her eyes. "I'm certain he never gave evidence against the Mafia to a Grand Jury," she said, "though I would never make fun of his delusions because they are so real to him." Suddenly tears appeared in her eyes and she said, "I'm so afraid he's on the brink of a relapse."

"In that case, you might want to contact Dr. Gomez. Perhaps he can do something to head it off? If you want to phone him from here, I will go downstairs and leave you to talk to him in privacy. It would be better to call him from here than from the Lopez home where Ted could eavesdrop on your conversation," Rhonda suggested.

"I may do that in a few minutes. I want to think about it and also pray about it first."

"Ginger, I know this is none of my business, but has he ever hit you or beaten you? I'm asking because he used to beat me with his fists until he was absolutely exhausted. I don't know why I didn't call the police. Why I put up with that is a mystery to me!"

"Living with a schizophrenic is nerve wracking to say the least," Ginger began. "Yes, he has beaten me several times, and I've put up with it, too. His behavior is unpredictable and frightening. He is suspicious and definitely prone to violence. In his defense, I must tell you that his delusions and his voices often cause his violent behavior. He believes that others plan to harm him and his voices tell him to fight back or to get them first."

"Do you think his schizophrenia could be caused because of his mother's desertion?" Rhonda inquired.

"No," said Ginger. "Definitely not. That's an out-dated belief. His early family life played no role in this disease. Schizophrenia is a biological brain disease. It's like his brain is broken or fragmented. Like he's dreaming when he's awake, and he had trouble distinguishing between reality and illusion. The disease could be caused by a chemical imbalance in the brain, but nobody yet knows for sure what causes it."

"Ginger, other than delusions and hallucinations, what are the symptoms of schizophrenia?"

"There is a list as long as your arm. Each person has a unique set of symptoms and nobody has every symptom. At times Ted withdraws, preferring to be alone. He will hibernate in his bedroom and not want me to come in. As you saw Saturday night he has problems in social functioning and he frequently displays disruptive behavior. He has problems concentrating and a lack of motivation which prevents him from being able to hold a job very long."

"When I knew him he had had four jobs in one year," Rhonda said, then thought a moment and continued, "I think he has a problem with grandiose delusions, too. I remember he told me he had been a Green Beret in Viet Nam, that he had swam in the Olympics, and that he had a fortune stashed in a Swiss Bank account. He even insisted that I memorize the box number and secret code."

"He still has grandiose delusions," said Ginger. "His most recent one was a humdinger. He told me he was the illegitimate son of the Duke of Windsor!"

"Ginger, you have your hands full, don't you?" Rhonda sympathized.

"Indeed I do. Some days it nearly gets the best of me, and I really need to talk to someone about it. That's why I'm so thankful that I can talk to you. You're the only person here in Guanajuato that I can talk to. I can't tell the Lopez family because I don't think they would understand. They would probably be frightened of him and kick us out! I want to stay with them because Ted does better in a structured home life setting than in a hotel."

"But do you think that's fair to the Lopez family? Don't you think they have a right to know that a potentially dangerous and violent man is staying in their home? Frankly, if I were in their place, I would certainly want to know. This is something you might want to talk over with Dr. Gomez."

"You're right, Rhonda, they should know. If you will excuse me, I will stay up here a few minutes and phone him. I think he will tell me the right thing to do. Also, he may be able to prevent Ted from having a relapse. Thank you so much for giving me his name and phone number."

Rhonda excused herself and went downstairs to give Ginger the privacy she needed. Eventually, she came downstairs, thanked Rhonda again and went on her way.

View of Guanajuato seen from Rhonda and Rick's home

# Chapter Eight

When Rhonda arrived at her classroom on Monday morning, Anita was waiting for her. "Can you have lunch with me today?" she invited. "I've asked Juanita, also."

"I'd love to," Rhonda said, accepting her invitation.

"See you after class, then," Anita said, and went on her way as the students began to arrive.

Several students gathered around Rhonda's desk and told her what a good time they had at her home and how much they liked her house. A couple said they had tried some of her recipes and that they were very good.

The bell rang and the students scurried to their desks. One of the girls named Marla raised her hand and asked where she could buy her cookbooks.

"I'll give a free book to everyone who makes an A in this class," Rhonda promised. "but for those who don't make an A, the books can be bought here at the University Bookstore and at the American Bookstores in Mexico City."

"I heard that you also write murder mysteries," said Tina.

"I've only written one: MURDER IN SAN MIGUEL," Rhonda said, "Now students, we had better get busy and learn some English."

When her two classes were over, Anita came to Rhonda's room and asked, "Ready for lunch?"

"You bet! I'm famished."

As they walked down the street to the Valadez Restaurant, one of Rhonda's favorite places to eat and fondly remembered as a hangout during her own college days at the University of Guanajuato, Anita said, "I have a lot of things to talk to you about. First, I owe you an apology for Ted's behavior at your party. I had planned to phone you and apologize earlier, but Ginger said she had already done so. I never was so embarrassed."

"It certainly was not your fault, Anita. You don't owe me an apology."

"But I was the one who asked if they could come," she said.

"Forget it, Anita. It was no big deal."

They arrived at the restaurant, met Juanita and found a table. They ordered enchiladas, melon and purified water. While they waited for their food, Anita continued, "I guess you noticed I wasn't at church on Sunday? Frankly, I was too embarrassed to go. I knew people would be asking me what is wrong with Ted. Well, I don't know what is wrong with him, but he must have some kind of a problem. I overheard them talking about his medication. Ginger was fussing at him because he hadn't been taking his pills. I wonder what kind of medication he's supposed to be taking? It must have something to do with his behavior. Is he on valium?"

Rhonda could truthfully reply that she didn't know. "Ginger has never told me the name of his medication. Why don't you ask her what he is taking and what it's for? She would probably tell you."

Just then the food arrived and Juanita ate a bite of the cheese enchiladas and murmured, "Umm...Delicious!"

They ate in silence for a few minutes, then Anita began to complain again. "They've been at my house for twelve days, twelve stressful days, and show no sign of leaving. I need peace. Ted keeps things stirred up. I wouldn't be surprised if we discovered that he is paranoid because he watches out the windows all the time like he's expecting to see someone out there spying on him. Even when we go somewhere in the car, he's always turning around, looking out the back window. He must think someone is following him."

"They'll probably be leaving soon," Rhonda said soothingly.

"I don't think so. Now, I'm not complaining about having Ginger. I enjoy having her and she could stay as long as she wanted to, but that Ted makes me nervous. By the way, I haven't told you the latest episode. Last night he got into an argument with one of my neighbors and punched him in the nose!"

"Oh no!" gasped Rhonda. "I see what you mean by stress. There's never a dull moment at your house!"

"That's for sure! And the neighbor threatened to sue Ted!" she laughed. "It's really not funny. It seems I'm spending a lot of time trying to appease people he has offended. Felipe tried to calm the neighbor, who was really irate and rightfully so. He finally talked the neighbor out of suing. He apologized to him and told him that Ted is taking some kind of medicine that has side effects that causes his strange behavior. I don't know how much longer I can stand him," she groaned.

"To change the subject," Rhonda said, "this is a big day at our house. Rick and I have been married twenty-four years today, and he is taking me for dinner at the Castillo de Santa Cecilia. I love that place."

"Yes, it's very picturesque, and is located in a small canyon near La Valenciana, which used to be the largest gold and silver producing mine in the world," Anita told her.

"I heard that the castle of Saint Cecilia was built nearly 300 years ago," said Rhonda. "Was it really a castle?"

"No, it was not a castle," Juanita said. "I'm not sure, but I think it was once a mine called the Santa Cecilia of the Nopal Mine. It does look like a castle, though."

"I remember going there years ago with Carlos. There were peacocks wandering around the garden and near the pool. I had my first and last tequila there. It was terrible!"

Juanita laughed. "I'll have to agree with you on that subject!"

Anita had her car and offered to drive Rhonda home. During the drive Anita said, "I hope you and Rick will come for dinner some night soon."

"We'd be happy to," smiled Rhonda, "as soon as your company leaves!"

# Chapter Nine

The phone was ringing when Rhonda walked into the house. She answered with the traditional Mexican greeting, "Bueno."

"Rhonda, is that you?" asked a familiar voice.

"It is," she replied.

"This is Anne. Didn't you recognize my voice?"

"Now I do, but when I answered I wasn't expecting to hear from someone from home. How are you? When are you coming to visit us?"

"That's what I've called about. Derek and I have Frequent Flyer tickets which we can use for Mexico and we thought we'd come down this weekend, if it's convenient?"

"Great! We'd love to have you come. We don't have a thing planned for this weekend. We'll take you on a tour of beautiful, picturesque Guanajuato! And you'll stay with us, of course."

"Wonderful! We should be there about two o'clock Saturday afternoon."

"We'll pick you up at the airport," Rhonda promised. "See you then."

When Rick came home she told him they were having company over the weekend, and he was pleased to learn that it was Derek and Anne Hall. "I could take them to Irapuato to play golf," he said.

"I promised them a tour of Guanajuato," she said. "Maybe we can do both."

They celebrated their anniversary at the Castillo de Santa Celicia that evening, and the dinner was excellent. "I'll bet Anne and Derek would like this place," said Rick. "Maybe

45

we'll bring them here Saturday night."

"Fine," Rhonda agreed, then said, "I had lunch with Anita today, and she's got her fingers crossed on both hands that her company will be leaving soon."

Rick grinned, "I saw Felipe and he told me about the latest incident. I guess you heard about it? Ted punched one of their neighbors."

"I heard about it," Rhonda nodded. "I feel sorry for all of them. Ted is an accident just waiting to happen!"

On Saturday afternoon Rick and Rhonda met the Halls at the airport, as promised. "Do you feel up to a tour or do you want to go home, unpack and put your feet up?"

"Do you think we're old since we're retired?" asked Derek. "We're raring to go sightseeing!"

After loading their suitcases into Rick's Ford Explorer, they started off on the tour. "Guanajuato was once Mexico's most prominent silver-mining city. It's a colonial town nestled in a valley between two high mountain ranges at 6,700 feet," Rick told them. "It has twisting quarry rock streets, pastel-walled houses, fifteen plazas, and a vast subterranean system of roads made from an old river bed."

"Hey, Rick, you're a pretty good tour guide. Where did you learn all of that?" teased Derek.

"I studied a tour book last night just to impress you," Rick grinned. "First we're going to stop at the La Valenciana Mine. It was discovered by a miner who later became the Count of Valenciana. In the mid 1500's it was the world's leading silver mine, and it's still being mined today. And over here," Rick pointed, "is the baroque church built by the Count. We'll also drive by his home."

"Let's take them for a ride on the Carretera Panoramica," suggested Rhonda, who then explained, "It's a road that skirts the town on surrounding mountain tops and provides a fantastic view of Guanajuato, and it's close to our house."

They exclaimed over the view as they rode, then Rick drove to the gigantic statue of the Pipila Monument, where he parked. They got out of the car and looked at the statue dedicated to a young soldier and hero of the War of Independence of 1810, and looked at the panoramic view of the city.

"This used to be a favorite parking place for the students," Rhonda said, "and it probably still is!"

"She and Carlos used to park here," teased Rick.

"How did you know?" she laughed.

"Rhonda said she had a dream about this place last year and said she saw flat land on the top of a mountain nearby that was for sale, so she bought it," said Rick.

"Yes, and my dream came true. The land we bought is nearby and it was the exact land I saw in my dream. It was flat land on top of a mountain near Pipila!"

"Since we're close to our house, we'll go home and drop off the suitcases, then continue the tour if you're not too tired," said Rick.

When they pulled up to the sidewalk in front of their home, Anne said, "I love your house! It's even prettier than the pictures you showed us."

"Thanks. Come on in and see it, "Rhonda invited them.

"I'll bet everyone loves the courtyard, don't they?" Anne asked as they walked through it.

"Yes, but courtyards are old hat around here. There's so many of them."

"But who else has a circular staircase and a circular tower room? My, I love it! It's like a mini castle!"

Rhonda laughed, "that's what Carlos calls it. We call it the "Hacienda de la Sierra Madre," These mountains are called the Sierra Madre which means Mother Mountains and since my mother left me the money that we used to build this house, it's named in her memory."

After putting their luggage in the guest bedroom, they drove to the Hacienda San Gabriel de la Barra and toured this REAL seventeenth century hacienda which contains formal rooms furnished with colonial antiques, gorgeous gardens, a pool and an ornate private chapel.

"How would you like to see a museum full of mummies?" Rhonda asked, after they finished touring the Hacienda.

"Sounds gross!" Anne said bluntly.

"Yes, but a trip to Guanajuato is not complete until you see them. It's a bizarre exhibition of mummified remains of human corpses. These were ordinary citizens who were buried in local soil containing minerals that preserved their bodies. Some are clothed. Others are as naked as jaybirds! They're really gruesome. Do you want to see them?" Rhonda asked.

"That's a privilege I can do without," Anne shuddered.

"I think I'll forego that pleasure, too," said Derek. "It doesn't sound like my cup of tea!"

Everyone laughed, and Rick said, "Let's eat. We can tour the down town area tomorrow."

"I think I've lost my appetite!" Anne groaned.

"You'll change your mind when you see where we're taking you," Rick assured them, then drove to the beautiful Castillo de Santa Cecilia.

On Sunday morning Rhonda prepared waffles and serve them in the courtyard with blueberry syrup. It's wonderful to eat in the open air on such a bright sunshiney day," Anne said.

"And it's wonderful to eat waffles that taste this good," Derek complimented her.

After breakfast they drove to the First Baptist Church of Guanajuato. When they went into their Sunday School class, they were surprised to see Ted and Ginger with Anita. They greeted them and introduced them to the Halls. Their teacher, Juanita Rios, tried her best to teach her carefully prepared lesson and control the class, but Ted, who apparently had again failed to take his medication, continually made inappropriate remarks. He topped himself when a comment was made about the American government and he said, "Did you know that the government uses radio waves to control people's minds?"

Everyone became quiet, not knowing what to say, because not only were they embarrassed for him, but they then understood that he had some kind of a mental problem.

When the class was over, they went into the sanctuary and heard an excellent sermon by the Reverend Felipe Lopez.

After church, they ate lunch at the second floor restaurant of the Hotel San Diego, located across from the main square, the Jardin de la Union. They sat at a table overlooking the zocalo, and ordered steaks prepared with garlic, roasted potatoes, sautéed vegetables and purified water to drink.

"I'm curious," Derek began, "about that guy in the Sunday School class named Ted. What is his problem?"

"He's mentally ill," Rhonda replied, then added piously, "and we should pray for him."

Rick changed the subject and suggested they go for a walking tour of Guanajuato after lunch.

After dessert and coffee, they began their tour from across the street at the main Plaza. Rick pointed out the ornate Juarez Theatre, across the street on Calle Sopena. "The theater was built as an opera house in 1903. Next to the theater is the Church of San Diego, which was built in 1633."

"This is a pretty little park," Anne said, pointing at the Jardin de la Union, a small triangular square with shady trees behind the benches. "I'll bet Rhonda and Carlos used to sit on those benches and listen to music of the mariachis playing there in that charming bandstand," she teased.

"You're right, we did!" grinned Rhonda. "It's a nice memory!"

Derek tactfully changed the subject and pointed up the hill above the theater and the church, "Is that the statue of Pipila up there that we saw yesterday?"

"Yes, it is," Rick answered. "Who wants to make the steep climb up the hill to it? It only takes an hour to climb it!"

"You can forget that!" laughed Anne. "I'm not wearing my walking shoes."

"Then let's walk to the Plaza de la Paz, just up the street, and see the beautiful baroque church, called the Basilica of Our Lady of Guanajuato, built in the 1600's. Inside is the famous statue of the Virgin of Guanajuato, which was presented to the town in 1557 by King Philip II of Spain because the town produced so much of the world's silver. Also, in this plaza you see the Count of Valenciana and Rul's mansion. He's the guy who owned the Valenciana silver mine that we saw yesterday."

They went inside the church to see the statue, then Rhonda suggested, "Let's walk on up the street to the street of the Kiss called in Spanish, the Callejon del Beso. "It's a narrow street about two feet wide that got it's name from the Romeo and Juiliet of Guanajuato. The girl's father didn't approve of the boy so they used to meet secretly on their separate balconies and kiss. One night the father caught them there and in a fit of anger he stabbed one of them. I think it was his daughter."

"It is the custom for the man to kiss his sweetheart when he comes to this street," Rick finished, leaning over and kissing Rhonda on the cheek.

After seeing the narrow street, Anne said, "I think we're going to have to have a driving tour of the rest of the town. My feet are hurting."

"Why don't you all sit in the park over there  called the Jardin Morelos," Rick said, pointing to it, "and I'll get the car and pick you up?"

"That sounds like a deal to me," said Anne.  She sat on the first bench she could find.

"We're going to Mexico City tomorrow.  Why don't you go with us, Rhonda?" she asked, after Rick had left.

"I'd love to, but I have to teach two classes every Monday," she said.

"I wish you could go.  But if you can't, why don't you give us Carlos' phone number, and we'll phone him and take him out to dinner one night while we are there?"

"Remind me to give it to you when we return to the house.  That's a great idea," Rhonda said, then added, "Talking about Carlos--this is another park with a memory of him.  This was where he first kissed me!"

Anne grinned, but didn't tease her.  Instead she said, "He's a very nice man.  Both Derek and I liked him when we met him at your house last Christmas."

"Rick and I both like him, too.  He's been a very good friend to both of us."

Rick soon arrived and they got into his car.  "I'm going to drive you past the University of Guanajuato where Rhonda teaches.  It's a white, castle-looking stone building with a baroque and Moorish facade," he said, pulling over to the curb in front of it.  "Also you might want to see the church next door to it.  I forgot what it's called."

"That's where I went to church when I went to the University here," said Rhonda.  "It's name is the Iglesia de la Compania de Jesus."

"Next, I'll show you the Alhondiga." he said.  Then they drove to the unadorned fortress-looking building.  "It was originally a granary, but later was used as a prison and a fortress during the Mexican Independence War. It was here that Pipila became a hero. Also, it was here that Father Hidalgo, who was the Father of the Mexican Independence movement, was beheaded and his head was put in an iron cage and displayed as a warning to the Mexicans. Today the Alhondiga is a museum."

"The Alhondiga has some terrific murals. I happened to be here when one of the murals was being painted and I used to go to the Alhondiga and watch the artist paint it," Rhonda said.

"There's a lot more to see, but you're probably getting tired of sight-seeing, so what do you want to do now?" Rick asked.

"Let's go back to your house and just relax," suggested Anne.

"Fine," agreed Rick and headed the car onto the subterranean road, Calle Miguel Hidalgo, built on the bed of a river which was diverted away because of the many floods it used to cause. Soon they were on Guanajuato Boulevard and at their home located along that street.

The next day when Rick was driving Derek and Anne to the airport, Rhonda asked where they were staying in Mexico City.

"We haven't made reservations anywhere yet. What hotel would you suggest?"

"The Maria Isabel Sheraton if you want to spend a lot of money. It's very nice and is located in the Santa Rosa shopping district. Two other less-expensive hotels we liked are the Maria Cristina and the Polanco."

"What places do you recommend we visit while we are there?" Derek asked.

"I wrote down a list for you," Rhonda said, giving him a piece of paper. "Be sure to see the Pyramids, the Bacilica of Guadalupe, Xochimilco Floating Gardens, Palacio de Bellas

Artes, Chapultepec Castle, the Archaeological Museum and the University of Mexico."

When they pulled into the parking lot of the airport, Rhonda said, "Why don't you stop back by here before you go home? Your visit was too short."

"We might do that," said Anne. "We'll call first before we come."

"Thanks for having us," said Derek. "We had a good time."

"We enjoyed having you. Come back anytime," said Rick.

"I wish you'd go with us," said Anne.

Later Rhonda wished she had gone with them, too. If she had, she would certainly have saved herself a lot of grief and embarrassment.

Valadéz Restaurant and the Juárez Theatre

Monument to Pipila, a hero of the War for Independence

The view of Guanajuato from Pipila

The Castle of Santa Cecilia

# Chapter Ten

Rhonda had spent the past week writing on her novel, titled MURDER IN THE POST OFFICE. It took place in Arkansas back in the early fifties.

The week had gone by without incident, then Anita phoned Rhonda. "I'm at the end of my rope!" she exclaimed. "Do you know that Ted and Ginger are still at my house? I don't think I'm ever going to get rid of them! Do you know they have been here for twenty six days! I'm ready to run away from home!"

"Anita, I think it's time you have a frank talk with them. Perhaps you ought to talk to Ginger first and tell her that you were wondering when they planned to return to the States. You might tell her that you love her, but Ted bugs you. If that doesn't work, you'll have to be even more blunt. Tell her that they have to leave by Wednesday. Some people don't take hints."

"I've been thinking about asking you a favor," said Anita.

"Oh? What's the favor?" asked Rhonda with trepidation.

"I know that you like Ginger, so I was wondering if you would invite them over to stay a few days with you?"

Rhonda laughed. "I'm sorry, I shouldn't have laughed. I can tell you feel strung out, and I'd feel the same way if they were staying with me."

"You didn't answer my question. Will you invite them to stay with you?"

"No way!" Rhonda refused adamantly. "No way! I couldn't stand it for even one day!"

"Neither can I! I can't wait until they leave!"

"Then either you or your husband are going to have to tell

them that they have to leave by Wednesday. Give them a deadline!"

"I have an idea," said Anita. "I'll tell them that they will need to leave on Wednesday, and that I want to give a farewell party for them on Tuesday night. How's that?"

"Why go to all that extra trouble? I'd just set the date for Wednesday and forget the party," Rhonda advised.

"No, I want to have a party for them. Will you and Rick come?"

"Frankly, Anita, I'd rather not."

"Rhonda, why don't you call Carlos and invite him to come to the party? I'll also invite Professor Almire and Juanita Rios. Perhaps I'll ask Dr. Gomez and his wife, too. Please say you will come."

"It's against my better judgment, but I'll come, if it's important to you. Also I'll phone Carlos tonight, but I doubt he will come since he's five hours away."

That evening at dinner she told Rick that they had been invited to dinner at the Lopez home. "I don't really want to go," she said.

"Then let's don't go, if you don't want to."

"Anita made me feel obligated to go," she said. "She told me to phone Carlos and invite him, too. She doesn't know him very well, so I don't know why she wanted him to come."

"The Beef Stroganoff is really delicious," Rick said, changing the subject. "I like it best when you make it with hamburger."

"Thank you," she said absentmindedly. She was silent a few minutes, thinking, then said, "I don't understand why Anita insisted on having a Bon Voyage party for Ted and Ginger. All she ever talks about is how she wishes they would leave. Now she wants to have a special dinner for them. I don't get it."

"She is probably feeling ashamed of herself for complaining so about her company, so now she wants to compensate by having a special dinner for them."

"You're probably right, Rick. If it's OK with you, I guess we ought to go. I'll call her and offer to bring dessert. Also, I'll phone Carlos. You don't care if he stays with us while he's here, do you? He probably won't even come, do you think?"

"You know I don't mind. Carlos is never any trouble."

After Rhonda finished the dishes, she phoned Carlos. When he answered she told him what she had phoned about. "Anita told me to phone you and ask you to come. I know it's a long way to come for a dinner party with people you hardly know, and I'll understand if you don't want to come, but if you do want to come, you are invited to stay with us."

"I wonder why she invited me?" he asked.

"I don't know. I wish she hadn't invited me. I don't want to go, because for some reason I have a really bad feeling about this dinner."

"You do?" Carlos asked.

"I certainly do."

"Then I am coming!" he exclaimed. "I had started to tell you that I couldn't come, but I have learned to respect your "feelings." When you say you have a bad feeling about something, something bad usually happens, so I think I'd better come. You might need me."

"Thank you. I feel better about it just knowing you are coming."

"My classes are over at the University at noon tomorrow, so I'll take the 1:00 bus and be there at 6:00."

"We'll pick you up at the bus station at 6:00. Thank you for coming. You're a good friend. Now I'd better hang up and call Anita. I'll tell her you are coming and see if she wants me to bring dessert."

"If she does I hope you take that delicious four layered chocolate cake with the crazy name! Now, what is it called?"

"Death by Chocolate!" Rhonda answered, laughing.

After they hung up, Rhonda phoned Anita and told her that Carlos would be there and that he requested that she bring a chocolate dessert that he particularly liked.

"Great! That will take care of the dessert," Anita said. "And I'm glad the three of you are coming. See you tomorrow night at 7:30."

Rhonda then went on into the kitchen and began to prepare Death by Chocolate.


### Beef Stroganoff

| | |
|---|---|
| 1 lb ground beef | 1 tsp salt |
| 3 slices diced bacon | 1/4 tsp paprika |
| 1/2 cup onion, chopped | 1/4 tsp pepper |
| 1 can mushroom soup | Hot cooked noodles |
| 1 can sliced mushrooms, drained | Dried parsley |
| 1 cup dairy sour cream | |

In skillet brown beef, bacon and onion. Add seasonings. Stir in soup and mushrooms. Cook slowly, uncovered, 20 minutes, stirring frequently. Stir in sour cream and heat. Serve over hot cooked noodles. Sprinkle with parsley. 4 servings.

# Death by Chocolate

1st layer:
1 cup flour                          1/2 cup pecans, chopped
4 Tbsp butter, melted

Mix together thoroughly and press in greased 9x13 inch pan. Bake 15 minutes at 350 degrees F. Cool completely.

2nd layer:
8 oz cream cheese, softened          1 cup powdered sugar

Beat until fluffy. Spread on first layer. Chill.

3rd layer:
2 (3 oz) pkgs chocolate              milk (quantity shown
  pudding mix                          on pudding pkg. less
1 tsp vanilla                          1/4 cup)

Cook pudding, milk and vanilla until thickened. Cool completely. Spread on second layer.

4th layer:
Cool whip                            pecans, finely chopped

Spread Cool whip over third layer. Sprinkle with nuts. Chill 4-6 hours before serving.

Basilica Colegiata de Nuestra Señora de Guanajuato

# Chapter Eleven

Since Rhonda didn't teach on Tuesdays she decided to go to her office and spend the day typing on her mystery novel. She had just finished chapter nine when the phone rang. It was Ginger. She hadn't heard from Ginger since the day she had come for lunch.

"Hi Ginger. It's good to hear from you."

"Thank you. I guess you know we are leaving tomorrow?" she asked.

"Yes, that's what Anita said when she phoned to invite me for your farewell dinner," Rhonda replied. "I'll miss you. I've enjoyed knowing you."

"Thank you," Ginger said. "Anita said you volunteered to bring dessert. What are you bringing?"

"It's a four-layer chocolate dessert. I hope you will like it."

"How do you make it?"

"The first layer is a crust made by mixing together 1 cup of flour, 4 Tablespoons of butter and 1/2 cup of chopped pecans, then you press this mixture into the bottom of a greased 9x13 inch pan and bake it for 15 minutes at 350 degrees. Cool it completely. Then for the second layer, you mix 8 oz. softened cream cheese with 1 cup of powdered sugar and beat it until its fluffy, then spread it over the cool crust. Place it in the refrigerator and chill it, then prepare the third layer by mixing together two small boxes of chocolate pudding mix with the amount of milk less 1/4 cup of the amount mentioned in the package directions. Mix the pudding until it's well blended, then stir in 1 teaspoon vanilla. Refrigerate the pudding until it's cold, then spread it over the second layer. For the fourth layer, just spread whipped cream over the whole dessert, then refrigerate it several hours or overnight before serving it."

"Oh, my!" Ginger exclaimed, sounding pleased, "it sounds delicious!"

"I'm so glad you approve," Rhonda said. "Have you eaten it before?"

"No, but it sounds divine!"

"Sometimes I sprinkle chocolate chips and chopped pecans over the top before I serve it. I think that makes it taste even better," said Rhonda.

"Oh no!" said Ginger. "Both Ted and I would like it better plain."

"All right, it's for you. If you want it to be plain, it will be plain!"

"Thanks, Rhonda. I'll see you tonight", she said and hung up.

Rhonda settled back down behind her typewriter, ready to write, but the ideas weren't coming. Oh, well, she thought, "I'll take Cleopatra for a walk and get a little exercise, then maybe I can type."

After their walk, she played ball with Cleopatra for a few minutes, then remembered that she had not changed the sheets on the guest bed. Camila didn't come on Tuesdays so Rhonda vacuumed and dusted the room for Carlos. She wondered when Rick would be home. He had gone to Irapuato to play golf with Carlos' uncle Guillermo. she hoped he would be home in time to pick Carlos up at the bus station. If not, she guessed she could take a taxi. She continued to think of things that needed to be done and never did get back to her novel. For some reason, she felt restless and couldn't seem to concentrate on her writing. Finally, she sat down with a good book and read until Rick came home. After he arrived and had showered and dressed it was time to pick up Carlos. They brought him back to their home and fixed him a coke, then just as they began to watch television, the phone rang and it was Dr. Gomez.

"Hi Rhonda," he said, "I meant to call you much sooner, but it's been busy around here. I'm calling because I thought you might like to ride to the Lopez house with us. No point in taking two cars when we're all going to the same place. Anita said Carlos might come, and if he does there's plenty of room for him, too."

"Thanks, Francisco. Sure, we'd be happy to ride with you. It's nice of you to ask," Rhonda replied. "By the way, I gave Ginger your phone number about two weeks ago and she talked like she was going to call you. I hope she did."

"She didn't," he said. "I've been rather concerned about her."

"That's really odd that she didn't phone, because I gave her your number and told her what you said, then I suggested she call from my office so that Ted wouldn't overhear her conversation, and I went out of the room to give her privacy to make the call. She stayed in there alone for quite awhile so I presumed she was talking to you, then she finally came downstairs, thanked me and left. I haven't seen her since."

"I suppose she has been making sure he takes his pill everyday, so he's probably doing OK and she didn't feel she needed to consult me," he said. "We'll be by to pick you up in thirty minutes, at 7:15, if that's OK?"

"We'll be ready," she said. "By the way, you did know I returned your book, didn't you? When I brought it to your house, your maid opened the door, so I gave it to her and she said she'd give it to you. It was very informative and I was interested in reading it. Thanks for the loan."

"Yes, she gave it to me," he said. "I'm glad you liked it. We'll see you in a few minutes. Adios!'

As they were all riding together to the Lopez home Rhonda asked the doctor if schizophrenics had to take pills or could injections be given.

"They can take injections," he answered. "If they often forget to take the pills a doctor can give them long-lasting injections once every two to four weeks."

"Since Ginger is a psych-nurse I assume she knows this, so I wonder why Ted hasn't had the injections?"

Francisco shook his head, "I don't know. I am concerned about him. Statistics show that in one year after leaving the hospital 70% of patients will have a relapse if they are not taking their medicine and being properly monitored."

"They've been here a month," Rhonda said. "We'll see what shape he's in tonight. Since I read the book you gave me, I understand his problem much better and now I empathize with him."

Rick asked, "Can schizophrenia be inherited?"

"Yes, it can," the doctor replied.

Rhonda said, "Then it's fortunate that they didn't have any children."

After they arrived and greeted everyone, Rhonda was especially pleased to see that Professor Almire was there. She shook his hand and told him how nice it was to see him again.

'I've meant to phone you and tell you what a good time I had at your party," he said, "So I am glad you are here so I can tell you now."

"You gave two great parties when I was in Guanajuato the first time, which I appreciated far more than I ever expressed."

Carlos, who was standing nearby, said, "It was at your first party that I met Rhonda."

Rhonda laughed, "Now, you can see why I'm so happy you gave that party! What would I have done without Carlos? He's the one who designed our house, you know. By the way I told him I wanted a courtyard like yours and also that I wanted to be able to sit on the roof like we could do at your house."

"Your courtyard is very elegant," he said. "Carlos, you did a wonderful job."

Before Carlos could thank him for the compliment, the maid came by with a tray of glasses of tomato juice. They all accepted a glass which tasted good with the cheese and crackers which Anita passed around. Rhonda noticed that Ginger was not in the room and that Francisco was talking to Ted, so she excused herself to join them. She heard Ted tell the doctor that he had been taking his medication each day, and that by some miracle the pills were no longer causing him to have the same side effects that he used to have.

"That's interesting," replied the doctor. "Would you mind telling me what side effects you used to have?"

"They were terrible. I used to feel like I was jumping out of my skin! I was restless and I was constantly pacing the floor."

The doctor nodded, "Akathisia, that is called. But you say the symptoms have completely stopped?"

"Yes, those symptoms have stopped, but now I have new ones. My legs cramp and hurt. Also I've had several upset stomachs. But that's probably from a case of turista," he said.

"Could I see one of your pills," the doctor asked.

"I don't know where they are," he said. "Ginger keeps them and gives me one each day. You might ask her."

"Ted, tell me how you are feeling. Are you going out every day?"

"No, I don't feel like going out. I stay home and watch television. I've been awfully tired lately."

"Do you sleep a lot?"

"I slept nearly all day yesterday, but I've only had a short nap today. My legs really hurt. Sleeping makes the pain go away."

"Don't you want to go sightseeing or out to a movie?"

"No, I want to stay here. You see, people are always talking about me, so I just stay here and watch TV. I've been receiving messages from the TV."

"What message have you been receiving?"

"That people want to hurt me."

Rhonda noticed that his facial and voice tone were expressionless. He almost talked in a monotone, showing little emotion, which was not like Ted. She remembered from reading the book about Schizophrenia that this could be a negative symptom called blunted affect which might indicate relapse. She wondered if she ought to mention it to Ginger, then decided that she ought to keep her nose out of their business. Her ears perked up though when she heard the doctor ask, "Do you get any other messages from the television set?"

"I certainly do. I was told not to use the phone because FBI agents are recording my phone calls. And there's one more thing. Anita gets very angry at me for unplugging the refrigerator, but you see I know it is a listening device used to eavesdrop on my thoughts."

Suddenly Ted began massaging his head quite vigorously.

"What are you doing Ted?" Rhonda asked.

"I'm trying to clear my head of unwanted thoughts."

"How do you feel?" she asked.

"Like rats are eating my brain."

"Oh Ted,. I'm so sorry. You see I never knew what your problem was, so I didn't understand. I wish I could help."

Suddenly he began quoting, "The mirror crack'd from side to side."

"Is that how your head feels?" she asked, sympathetically."

"My brain is fragmented like a mirror crack'd," he said, looking woebegone.

Rhonda put her hand on his shoulder, then he grabbed her hand and shoved it away and screamed, "Don't touch me!"

"Oh my," she said, "I'm sorry." Embarrased, she excused herself and went into the kitchen to see if there was anything she could do to help.

"What's wrong with Ted?" Anita asked. "He sure has a short fuse."

"I inadvertently upset him. I didn't mean to," Rhonda replied. "Perhaps Ginger can calm him. Where is she?"

"She's still in her room. Dressing, I guess," Anita replied. "Would you mind telling her dinner is about ready? It's the last room on the left."

"Sure," Rhonda said, then left to find Ginger. She knocked on the bedroom door and said, "Ginger, dinner is about ready."

"I'll be there in a minute," Ginger replied, not opening the door or inviting Rhonda inside. As Rhonda started to return to the kitchen she had to pass through the living room and she noticed Ted had calmed down and was sitting quietly on the couch beside Dr. and Mrs. Gomez, drinking some tomato juice.

Just then Anita appeared in the living room and said, "Dinner is ready. Please come into the dining room now." As she made this announcement Ginger appeared and then Anita seated husbands and wives together at the table.

First, the maid served the vegetable soup, bread and butter.

Ginger asked Carlos, "How long have you known Rhonda?"

"Thirty-five years," he replied. "We met here when she attended the University of Guanajuato."

"And you've continued to be friends during these past thirty-five years?"

"We hadn't seen each other for thirty years, then when

Rick and Rhonda decided to come to Mexico, Rhonda wrote to me. When they came, we were like the three musketeers. Together everyday. Then they invited me to spend Christmas at their home, which I did."

"And they asked you to design their home?" she asked.

He nodded, "Yes. Do you like it?"

"It's beautiful," she said. "So unique."

"Thank you."

The maid took the empty soup bowls away, and returned with a platter of spaghetti for each person.

Before Rhonda touched her water she asked, "Anita, is this purified water?"

"Absolutely," she replied. "That's the only kind we ever drink. We're as afraid to drink tap water as you are."

"Rhonda sipped her water then and said, "It's so nice of you to have us for dinner."

"You're welcome anytime," Anita replied.

Rhonda smiled at her, then turned to Dr. Gomez, "I'm always interested in how people meet. Where did you meet your wife?"

"We were students together at the University. How did you meet Rick?"

"At a party. A mutual friend who was also there introduced us."

Rick turned to Anita. "How did you and Felipe meet?"

"At his church. I graduated from college in the states and had attended the Baptist Church there with Ginger. You did know she and I were room mates our senior year?"

"Yes," Rick nodded.

"Then when I returned to Guanajuato, I decided to continue attending the Baptist Church."

"It was destiny!" Felipe exclaimed, continuing the story.

"I was standing at the pulpit when she came in and sat down. Right then I thought to myself, 'That's the girl for me!'"

"After the service was over," Anita said picking up the story, "he stood by the front door shaking hands with each person as they left. When he shook my hand, I said, "My name is Anita Rivera, and I enjoyed your sermon."

Felipe continued, "And I asked her if she was married. She shook her head, said no, and then I asked her to have lunch with me."

Professor Almire laughed and said, "You didn't waste any time, did you?"

"Not much!" Felipe grinned. "We were married six months later. How about you?"

"I met my first wife at the doctor's office in the waiting room. We both had the flu!"

Everyone chuckled, imaging them sitting together, coughing and blowing their noses.

Just then the maid removed their plates, and replaced them with plates of chicken, rice, asparagus and sliced melon. She poured more water, tea and coffee.

"Delicious," murmured Marta, finishing a bite of pollo y arroz, chicken and rice.

"Thank you," Anita said.

"Just wait until you see the four layered chocolate dessert," Carlos told her. "Rhonda brought it."

"I love chocolate," Marta smiled. "My mouth is watering already."

"Mine, too," said Juanita. "There's nothing better than chocolate."

Rhonda noticed that Ted hadn't said a word during the dinner, though he was eating heartily. She turned to Dr. Gomez and asked, "Did you know Ted is a poet? He writes wonderful poems. And songs, too."

Felipe said, "Ted, you've been hiding your light under a bushel! If I'd known you were a poet, I'd have asked you to write a poem about my sermon and I'd have read it in church."

"Perhaps I can write one later tonight for the sermon this coming Sunday," he offered.

"That would be great. My sermon is about David and Bathsheba."

"I'll give the poem to you before we leave tomorrow," Ted said. "It will be a small thank you for having us here."

"How nice, Ted," murmured Anita feeling bad about all the negative remarks she had made about him.

The maid came in, removed their dinner plates, placed dessert in front of each guest, then refilled water glasses, coffee and tea cups.

Marta was the first to exclaim that the cake was delicious. "I certainly want your recipe, Rhonda." She turned to her husband and asked, "Don't you think it's delicious, Francisco?"

"I love it," he said. "Maybe you could serve it when Mother comes to visit."

Just then Marta Gomez exclaimed that her pearl and diamond earring had fallen off her ear. Everyone pulled back their chairs and began to look under the table to help her find it. Finally Dr. Gomez found it under his chair. While the flurry was going on, Rhonda subconsciously noticed that Ted sprinkled something over his dessert.

After dessert and coffee, they sat around the table talking for awhile. Finally, Anita suggested, "Why don't we move into the living room where it's more comfortable?"

After everyone had been seated, Anita passed around some homemade mints. "Good," said Rick, taking a second one.

A few minutes later, Ted stood and said, "Please excuse me."

"Don't you feel well?" Dr. Gomez inquired.

"Just tired. I think I'll lie down awhile," Ted said, and left the room.

"I hope he's OK, " Anita said. "Do you think you ought to check on him, Ginger?"

Ginger stood, mumbled that she'd be back soon, and then followed Ted from the room. She was only gone a few minutes. When she returned she said, "I think he's just tired, but perhaps I ought to give him an aspirin. I'll get some water." She disappeared into the kitchen and soon returned with a glass of water, then carried it to Ted's room.

Rhonda couldn't resist teasing Anita. "He might be too sick to leave tomorrow, and have to stay another week or two."

"That would be my luck," grinned Anita.

Ginger had been sitting on a small sofa with Rhonda. Since that space was now vacant, Carlos went over and sat by her.

"Hi Beauty," he said in a low voice so others wouldn't hear.

"Hi Handsome," she grinned. "By the way, why do you call me that name? I like it, of course."

"Because I think you're beautiful."

"You know what to say to make my day, don't you?" she asked, smiling.

"My dad called my mother 'beauty'," he said.

"Carlos, you're a case!" she chuckled, then changed the subject. "By the way, did Derek and Anne Hall phone you when they were in Mexico City?"

"Yes, they did. We had lunch together, then I took them for a tour of Chapultepec Castle."

About that time Ginger came back into the room. "I think he's OK," she said as she sat down in the chair Carlos had vacated. "But he has a stomach ache."

Carlos reached into his pocket and pulled out some pills. "Give these Pepcid pills to him. They're good for stomach

73

aches."

Anita suggested, "Let's bow our head and pray that God will heal Ted of his illness."

Rhonda grinned to herself, knowing Anita had an ulterior reason for praying.

After the prayer, Professor Almire said he had better go home. "Not as young as I used to be," he joked.

Soon the others began to leave so Dr. Gomez asked Rick if he was ready.

"I think so," Rick replied.

Rhonda turned to Ginger and said, "I'll phone you in the morning to say goodbye and to hear how Ted is feeling."

Everyone thanked Anita and Felipe for a delicious dinner and a lovely evening.

When Rhonda, Rick and Carlos were seated in the Gomez' car, Fernando said, "Parties may overwhelm a schizophrenic person. Groups may be stressful and make him nervous. Ted will probably be OK now that we have all left."

Later they learned that Dr. Gomez missed the mark with that comment.

# Chapter Twelve

The phone rang, awakening Rick and Rhonda.

"Who on earth can be calling at this hour?" Rick sleepily complained.

"I'll get it," Rhonda said since the phone was on the nightstand beside her side of the bed. Taking the phone off the hook she answered, "Bueno."

In an aside to Rick she whispered, "It's Ginger."

"What did you say, Ginger? Would you repeat that? You can't be serious! Ted's dead! What happened? Poisoned? I can't believe it! Where are you? The hospital! Do you want us to come? What can we do to help you? Sure. We'll be there. At the hospital or the Lopez' home? OK. We'll see you in a few minutes. Bye."

She hung up the phone and said, "Rick, she wants us to go to the Lopez' home. We'd better get up and get dressed."

"What time is it?" Rick asked, yawning.

"5:30 A.M.," Rhonda replied, glancing at the clock on the night stand. "She said Ted is dead, that he was poisoned. They are leaving the hospital and she wants us to come to the Lopez home."

"At this hour?" he mumbled, drowsily.

"That's what she said."

"She's hysterical. I'll call Felipe and find out what's going on. What's his number?" he asked yawning again.

Rhonda opened the top drawer of the nightstand and took out the telephone directory, looked up the phone number and gave it to him.

Rick phoned Felipe, who said if it wasn't too much trouble, Ginger did indeed want the three of them to come to his house as soon as possible.

"We'll be there in a few minutes," Rick said, then hung up the phone and told Rhonda to wake up Carlos.

She put a negligee over her night gown, then went to Carlos' door and knocked. "I'm awake," he said. "Come in." She entered the room and he said, "The phone woke me. What has happened?"

"Ginger called from the hospital and said Ted had died from poisoning. That's all I know, but they want us to come to the Lopez home."

"I'll be ready in five minutes," he said.

It was about 6:00 A.M. when the three of them arrived at Anita and Felipe's home and were invited inside. They were seated in the living room where Ginger was dissolved in tears.

"I can't believe he's gone!" she cried. "What will I do without him?"

"I'm so sorry," Rhonda said.

Felipe said, "The hospital called and they want to do an autopsy."

"An autopsy?" wailed Ginger. "No, no! I won't let them cut him up. I refuse to allow it!"

"I don't think we have a choice in the matter. They said two policemen are coming here to talk to us. We needed you three here for moral support," said Anita.

"We're happy to do anything we can," Rhonda said. "But I don't understand what's going on. Can you tell us the whole story of what has happened?"

Felipe said, "You know Ted left to go to his room. He said he wasn't feeling well. Apparently, he gradually felt worse, becoming nauseous and had a painful stomach ache. When I was called in to see him, at 4:00 A.M., he was bent over in pain and was in the bathroom throwing up. Ginger had given him the Pepcid pills that you gave her, Carlos, a couple of hours earlier, but they didn't seem to be working, so I gave him a big dose of Pepto Bismol.

By 4:30 in the morning he was almost screaming with pain. Ginger was in tears. She had done everything she knew to do to make him comfortable, so we decided to take him to the hospital emergency room. When we got him there he was sweating, his throat was burning, his stomach was killing him. Just as we entered the hospital, he threw up again so they hurriedly took him to an examination room where he continued having severe gastrointestinal problems. The doctor wasn't sure what was wrong and asked what he ate for dinner. He finally decided the problem was Salmonella, E. coli bacteria or Ptomaine poisoning, thinking that he got a bad piece of chicken. However, none of us were ill, so I don't see how it could be the chicken.

Finally they called in a poison expert, but Ted died while he was examining him."

Ginger began to cry and wring her hands. "Oh Ted, Ted, please don't leave me," she sobbed. "How can I bear it! I can't live without you."

"Shouldn't you go to your room and lie down?" Rhonda asked her.

"No, I'll be OK," Ginger replied, tears running down her cheeks.

"Didn't the doctor give him anything to counteract the poison? That is, if it was poison," Carlos asked.

"I guess they had to know what kind of poison it was in order to know what to give him, and that was why they called in the poison expert," Ginger said.

Just then the doorbell rang and two policemen were escorted into the living room. They introduced themselves as Agente Sola and Agente Alcocer.

Anita explained to the policemen that three of the people

present did not speak Spanish, but that she or Carlos could act as interpreter.

One of the policemen, Agente Sola, took out his notebook and asked each person for their name, address, phone number, age, etc. then wrote down the information.

When he was finished, Agente Alcocer said, "We will be investigating the death of Ted Saxon. At first the attending doctor thought he was ill from Salmonella poisoning, but the poison expert thinks differently and has ordered a series of tests.

First, please tell me what Señor Saxon ate for dinner."

Anita replied, "Tomato juice, cheese and crackers before dinner. Vegetable soup, spaghetti, melon, chicken, rice, asparagus, bread, butter, a chocolate dessert, and coffee to drink." However all of us ate the same food and none of us are sick."

"Apparently he ate one thing that nobody else ate," muttered Carlos.

"Do you have a garbage disposal, Senora Lopez?" asked Agente Sola.

"Si, but it's on the blink, so I still have the table scraps if you want to analyze them?" she offered.

She went into the kitchen and he followed, watching her dump the plate leavings from a pan onto a large piece of extra duty foil, wrap it securely, then place it in a grocery bag. "Do you want it now or later?" she asked.

"Later, is fine," he said. "Would you please place it in the refrigerator until we are ready to go?"

After she refrigerated it, they returned to the living room in time to hear Agente Alcocer say, "Nobody should leave town until the results of the tests are in, or until you have permission from the ministerio público, the police station."

That announcement was met with silence.

"Let's get some background information," Agente Sola suggested. "We'll start with you, Señora Saxon. First let me express my deepest sympathy."

Ginger nodded and murmured, "Thank you."

"Please tell us about your husband, his background, education, occupation, all pertinent information."

"He was born in Kansas 59 years ago. His parents divorced, and his mother re-married then left him and his brother to be raised by their maternal grandmother, who didn't want the responsibility.

He only had two years of college, then dropped out to join the army. It was about this time that he was diagnosed with paranoid schizophrenia. He has been in and out of hospitals since he was 24. He has been married three times. His first wife divorced him. Schizophrenics can be abusive, unpredictable, and they're very difficult to live with. He knew that and didn't blame her. His second wife died ten years ago, and he and I have been married one year. He had no children, his grandparents and parents are dead. He's had no communication with his brother in over twenty years, and he had almost no friends. I've done my best to take care of him. I don't know what I'll do without him," she said, as tears began to flow down her face.

Anita went over to her and patted her shoulder in a comforting gesture, and Carlos gave her his handkerchief.

The Agente then turned to Reverend Lopez and asked, "What can you tell us about him? He has been a guest at your home for a few days?"

"For a month!" Anita interrupted.

Reverend Lopez said, "Ted seemed like a nice man. He was somewhat withdrawn and spent much of his time either watching TV or sleeping. He seemed very jealous of his wife. If he thought anyone stared at her, he became quite belligerent, sometimes even threatened to fight the person.

He sometimes seemed suspicious, even paranoid, thinking people were following him, watching him or talking about him.

I think he might have been abusive to his wife. More than once I overheard scuffling then crying, which caused my wife and me to think he was abusive toward her. We didn't want to interfere, yet thought if he were beating her that we should. We were in an uncomfortable situation."

The policeman turned to Ginger and asked, "Was your husband abusive to you?"

Ginger hung her head and murmured in a low voice. "Yes, at times he was, but I don't think he meant to be. He was always so sweet and apologetic to me afterwards. He was a very dear man and I loved him so much."

Agente Sola said, "Señora, you should have made a formal complaint against him."

"Please Señor," she said, "Let's don't talk about him like this. It upsets me. He was a good man most of the time."

Anita said, "Rhonda was acquainted with him in his younger days."

Rhonda looked at her, frowned and silently mouthed the word, "Thanks."

Agente Sola said, "Señora Winters, please tell us what you knew about Senor Saxon."

"He was about 26 years old when I knew him. He could be charming and he could be abusive. I also saw paranoid actions. He often thought people were spying on him. He couldn't keep a job. He liked to gamble and drink, but eventually he began going to church and became a Christian. However, he continued to be abusive, and I stopped seeing him."

"What do you mean by abusive?" asked Señor Sola.

"When he became angry he would hit me, throw things and have a tantrum. He once pointed his .357 magnum at my head and threatened to shoot me. Another time he cut my arms with a glass and I had to have fourteen stitches. These things happened at the end of our friendship. He was very nice to me at first."

"Was he jealous toward you, also?" asked Agente Alcocer.

"Yes. Very jealous. Once when I made an appointment with a male hair stylist, he went with me and stuck with me like glue. When we left he threw a fit simply because I had gone to a shop owned by a man. He shoved me across the floor yelling, "Don't go back there." Afterwards he would be sorry and loving. Guess that's called mood swings?"

He turned to Ginger and asked, "Did he treat you the same way?"

She nodded. "His behavior was unpredictable."

"I'll need a list of the names of your dinner guests and the seating arrangement at the dining table," said Agente Sola.

"Who sat beside the Senor at dinner?" he asked.

"Anita and Ginger. Rhonda and Rick sat across the table from him." Reverend Lopez replied.

Agente Alcocer turned to Anita. "Who cooked the dinner, Senora?"

"I cooked most of it. My maid helped some. She prepared the spaghetti, the tea and coffee. Also she went to the bakery and purchased the rolls and she served the dinner. Rhonda brought the dessert."

He turned to Rhonda and asked, "What dessert did you bring?"

"It was a four layered chocolate dessert with a crust as the first layer, a cream cheese filling as the second layer, chocolate pudding as the third layer, and it was topped with whipped cream as the fourth layer."

"And what is the name of this delicious-sounding dessert?" he asked her, smiling.

Her reply knocked the smile off of his face.

She said, "It's called Death by Chocolate."

The Street of the Kiss
Callejón del Beso

# Chapter Thirteen

Since neither Carlos, Rick nor Rhonda were sleepy after they were allowed to return home, Rick suggested, "Let's sit at the kitchen table and do some brainstorming. It might help. We don't have a shred of evidence."

"Good idea," Carlos agreed.

"I'll run upstairs and get paper and a pen," Rhonda said. "Be right back."

They sat around the table and Rhonda wrote the five W's: Who, What, Why, When and Where.

1. Who died? Ted.
2. What killed him? Probably poison
3. Why was he killed? Unknown
4. When did he die? This morning 3/25/98.
5. Where was he poisoned? Probably dining room of the Lopez home.

Next she wrote: Motive, Means and Opportunity. "First, what was the motive?" she asked, then wrote down each person's reply.

1. Motive: He was abusive, hard to get along with and live with. He had a short fuse. Domineering, might have knowledge or know secrets that someone didn't want told.

He probably wasted Ginger's money, may have gambled away his own salary when he worked.

He had no money, so he wasn't killed for his money unless he had taken out a life insurance policy at sometime. Or possibly he did have a fortune in a Swiss bank, but that's highly unlikely."

"Now let's discuss MEANS." then she wrote on the paper.
2. Means and below that 3. Opportunity.

2. Means- probably poison. Could be accidental poisoning. Could be murder.

3. Opportunity- Anyone at the party could have poisoned him either as he sat in the living room drinking the tomato juice and eating cheese and crackers, or at the dinner table as he ate his food.

Carlos asked, "Couldn't he have been slowly poisoned for several days and then died after the dinner because by then he had ingested enough to kill him?"

"That's a possibility," agreed Rick. "I read about a case like that."

"Now shall we discuss suspects?" asked Rhonda. "I'll write down the names of the eleven dinner guests, then we can write a motive by each person's name."

"You only have ten suspects," Carlos pointed out.

"True," said Rhonda, "if suicide has been ruled out. But can we rule it out? I just remembered something. Last night I saw Ted sprinkle a packet of sugar over his dessert. But how do we know there was sugar in the packet? This is far-fetched, but what if he had been slowly poisoning himself?"

"What would be his motive?" asked Rick.

"Possibly his illness," replied Rhonda. "He has probably been mentally ill since he was around twenty years old. I read somewhere that 10-15% of schizophrenics commit suicide. Perhaps Ted could tell he was about to relapse, and he didn't want to be hospitalized again. Perhaps he was sick and tired of it all and decided to end it. However I doubt that he killed himself, but I am going to write his name as suspect # 1.

| Suspects | Motive |
|---|---|
| 1. Ted | Suicide. Depression. He was at a low point in his life, and probably on the verge of a relapse. |

| 2. Ginger | His abusive behavior. Wasted her money. To get his life insurance and money from secret Swiss account if he had one. To put him out of his misery. Perhaps she had secrets he had threatened to tell. |
|-----------|-----------------------------------------------------|
| 3. Felipe | No motive |

Before asking anyone if they thought Felipe had a motive, Rhonda wrote "No motive" by his name.

Carlos objected, "What if he did have a motive? What if he was in love with Ginger and he decided to get rid of his competition? She is an attractive woman."

Rick shook his head. "Felipe is a minister. A man of God. He would never do that. Besides even with Ted dead, he would still be a married man. So is he going to poison Anita next?"

"You never know a person," said Rhonda. "Carlos is right. He should be a suspect. Remember all the preachers we've heard about who have had affairs?" She then wrote Felipe's name again, but left it blank. We'll fill it in when we have facts or at least a good clue as to what his motive might be. Next is Anita."

| 3. Felipe | |
|-----------|---|
| 4. Anita | She didn't like Ted. She knew he was abusive to her friend Ginger. She cooked dinner and had opportunity. |
| 5. Carlos | Gave Ted some capsules. Were they Pepcid pills or poison? |

Carlos laughed, "Rhonda everytime I get around you, I become involved in a murder investigation!"

"Twice in less than a year!" Rhonda grinned. "At least your life has not been boring!"

Rick said, "Rhonda write down your name for number 5. I suspect you are seriously going to be considered as a prime suspect."

She nodded, "I know," then wrote down her name and possible motives.

6. Rhonda

Ted knew her secret. She did not want people to know he was her ex-husband. Perhaps she still hated him because of his brutality and because he wasted much of her money and because he had embarrassed her so many times. She had opportunity. Not only had she made the cake, but she sat across the table from him.

7. Rick

"Who can think of a motive for Rick? "Rhonda asked. She grinned at him and said, "Still water runs deep!"

"Perhaps I resented the way he has treated you and I decided to finish him off," Rick suggested jokingly.

8. Dr. Gomez

9. Marta Gomez

10. Juanita Rios

11. Professor Almire

"I have thought of a twelfth suspect," said Carlos. "The maid! But I can't think of a motive for any of these people. Perhaps when we know them better, we will discover one.

12. Maid, Alejandra

Now, let's draw the seating arrangement at the table.

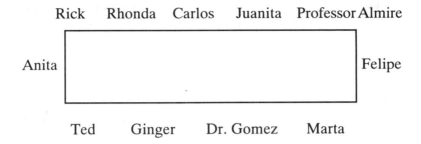

Rick observed, "Those closest to Ted were: Anita, Ginger, then Rick and Rhonda. It would be fairly easy for either Anita or Ginger to slip something into Ted's drink or his food, but quite difficult for any of the others.

Soon after Rhonda had finished drawing the sketch of the table and where each guest had sat, the phone rang. Since she was closest to the phone she picked it up and said "Bueno."

"Hi Rhonda, this is Javier Valdez."

"Well, hello Comandante!" she greeted him, pleased to hear from him.

"Ordinarily I wouldn't be interfering in Agentes Sola and Alcocer's investigation, but since you and I are neighbors and since I had that conflict with Ted Saxon at your home, I thought I would call, if you don't mind."

"I'm very pleased that you phoned, Javier," she replied. "It was a shame about Ted."

"Was it?" he asked. "I don't know. Maybe it was a blessing. I was informed that he was paranoid-schizophrenic with a very poor prognosis of ever recovering. He couldn't have been very happy, always thinking the Mafia was trying to assassinate him, and hearing voices in his head screaming obscenities and telling him he's no- good. Then he had delusions that caused him nothing but trouble. That man had so many positive and negative symptoms that his life must have been miserable."

"Yes, but he was newly married and seemed to be happy with her," said Rhonda. "So I hope he had some happiness in his life."

"The cause of his death is under investigation. I understand you were at the dinner where he was when he became ill?"

"Yes, unfortunately, I was there, and now I'll be considered a suspect because I made the dessert." She sounded irritated.

He laughed. "Everyone there may be considered a suspect."

"Do they know what caused his death yet?" she asked.

"No. It will probably be two or three days before we know. Do you want me to call you with the report?"

"Sure. I'd be interested," she said. "By the way, Rick, Carlos and I have been sitting here at the kitchen table playing detective. We've made lists of suspects, motives, opportunity, means, etc. And while we were talking the case over, I remembered something that I ought to tell you. I vaguely remember Ted sprinkling a packet of sugar over the top of his dessert. I overheard Ginger say he liked his coffee extra sweet. Perhaps he carried sugar packets in his pocket to make it sweeter. Do you think there's any chance he poisoned himself, that it wasn't sugar in the packet?"

"Who knows?" he said. "But this information might be helpful. I'll phone Sola and Alcocer. They can check out that angle."

"Someone could have "doctored" the sugar packet before he sprinkled the contents over his food," Rhonda suggested then added, "if he did".

"That's another point to consider. Thanks, Rhonda. You've been helpful. I'll call you when I know something. Adiós!"

After she hung up, she went into the kitchen and prepared

lunch.

"You two are going to like this casserole," she told, Rick and Carlos, "but it's high in fat, so I'm serving small portions!"

"What are the ingredients?" Carlos asked. He liked to cook and sometimes when he visited them he helped Rhonda cook dinner.

"It contains hamburger, onion, cheez whiz, mushroom soup, chili powder, garlic, crushed Fritos and hominy. It tastes a lot better than it sounds."

"Can I help you?" he asked.

"Sure. Would you slice this cantaloupe and some fresh limes?" she asked, giving it to him.

After she put the casserole into the oven, she mixed up some chocolate chip cookies and baked them for dessert.

They ate lunch in the open air courtyard, shaded by the Eucalyptus tree growing in the center. "This casserole is delicious," Rick said, reaching for a second portion.

"I'll have some more of that, too," said Carlos. "I love it!"

"I'm glad," she smiled as she squeezed fresh lime juice over her melon. "In a minute I'll take the cookies out of the oven. They're always best when they're hot."

After eating a half dozen cookies and finishing his tea, Carlos suggested, "Let's go to a movie and get our minds off of Ted."

## Hominy-Cheese Casserole

1 small jar jalapeno Cheez Whiz
3 teaspoons chili powder
1 teaspoon garlic salt
1 chopped onion
1 can mushroom soup

1/2 pound ground beef-
browned and drained
4 cans drained hominy
1 cup crushed Fritos
corn chips

Heat Cheez Whiz, onion, soup, chili powder and garlic salt until boiling.
Combine hominy and beef. Pour cheese mixture over hominy and beef. Mix well. Place in 9x13" greased casserole. Top with crushed Fritos. Bake at 350 degrees F for 20 minutes.

## Chocolate Chip Oatmeal Cookies

1 cup butter
1 cup brown sugar
1/2 cup granulated sugar
2 eggs
2 Tablespoons milk
2 teaspoons vanilla
1 3/4 cups flour

1 teaspoon baking soda
2 1/2 cups uncooked
oatmeal
1 12 ounce package
semi-sweet chocolate
chips

Heat oven to 375 degrees F. Beat together butter and sugars until creamy. Add eggs, milk and vanilla and beat well. Add combined flour, and baking soda, and mix well. Stir in oatmeal and chocolate chips; mix well. Drop by rounded tablespoonfuls onto ungreased cookie sheet. Bake 9 to 10 minutes. Cool 1 minute on cookie sheet; remove to wire rack. Makes about 5 dozen.

# Chapter Fourteen

Two days later, true to his word, Comandante Javier Valdez phoned with news.

"Hi Rhonda," he greeted her, "the lab has finished analyzing Ted's bodily fluids and stomach contents. Wouldn't you hate to earn a living that way?" he groaned.

"That's for sure!" she replied, trying not to laugh at his comment.

He continued, "His symptoms pointed to poison. His autopsy was done this morning and I just got the report about an hour ago. The pathology lab had been running tests for a variety of poisons. We also have received the lab analysis of the food he had eaten. Apparently he was murdered due to arsenical poisoning. There was quite a bit of poison in his blood, so he only lived about nine hours after ingesting it."

He continued, "I'll read part of the report to you. The white crystalline powder prepared from true arsenic is one of the most deadly poisons known. It is used mostly for pesticides and herbicides, but also in manufacture of ceramics, paint, wallpaper and rat poisons.

Arsenic poisoning causes severe gastric distress, esophageal pain, vomiting and bloody diarrhea. The skin is cold and clammy and blood pressure plummets followed by convulsions and coma."

Rhonda shuddered, "How awful. Whoever did this must have hated him a lot to make him suffer like that."

"True," he agreed. "By the way, if you three sleuths have come up with any more ideas about "Whodunnit," I'd be interested."

"We haven't a clue," Rhonda replied, then an idea suddenly popped into her head. "However there was a diversion at the dinner table that night which I'd forgotten all about until now. Marta Gomez lost her pearl and diamond earring that evening while we were eating dessert. Everyone pulled back their chair and looked under it and under the table in an effort to help her find it. Eventually, Dr. Gomez found it under his chair, and returned it to her."

"What you are saying, I presume," Javier asked, "is that this diversion could have given the killer an opportunity to sprinkle the arsenic over the dessert?"

"Absolutely," Rhonda replied, "and wouldn't you know they would be eating my dessert at the time! Presumably arsenic is a white powder and it could have been sprinkled over the white whipped cream and Ted would not have noticed anything unusual about the appearance of the dessert."

"Did anyone get up and pass by Ted's chair?" he asked.

She thought a minute, then answered, "I'm not sure. It does seem to me that someone did get up, but I can't remember who, and I can't remember if they passed by Ted.

"Can you hold the phone a minute and I'll ask Carlos and Rick if they remember?"

When she asked them, they were in the same boat with her. They vaguely remembered people moving around, but couldn't remember who as they had their minds on finding the earring.

She reported this information to the police chief and he said, "Sola and Alcocer will need to ask this question of the other guests and the hosts, too. Hopefully someone will remember seeing who might have moved from their chair. The search may have given opportunity to several people."

"You might have the police or agentes talk with the maid also," Rhonda suggested. "She might have seen something that the others missed as she was serving the food."

"I'll do that. Good idea!" he said. "If you think of anything else that might be helpful to the case, please call me."

"Oh by the way," he added, "would you mind if agente Sola came to your home to discuss with you what you've told me? Carlos could translate for you."

"I'd be happy for him to come," she replied.

Later that day, Agente Sola came to Rick and Rhonda's home. "It has come to my attention that you have remembered a couple of occurrences during the fatal dinner, and I'd like for you to tell me about them," he said then Carlos translated.

"Are you talking about the earring which was dropped during dinner?" Rick asked.

"Yes, that, and also about Ted sprinkling something over his food."

Rhonda explained, "Just as we started to eat dessert, Marta Gomez lost an expensive earring. Apparently it fell off her ear and onto the floor. Earrings do that sometimes without any help from their wearer. All the guests were looking for it under their chairs and under the table. It seems to me that one or two people or more arose from their chairs to look around the floor, as it could have rolled away from the table. But I honestly don't remember who got up."

"Did anyone pass by Ted's chair?" he asked.

"I'm not sure. My attention was focused on finding the earring. The other two things were seen more sub-consciously. Now when I think back about it, I vaguely remember someone getting up and moving around. I also vaguely remember Ted sprinkling something on his dessert because I thought it was an odd thing for him to do. Hopefully one of the other guests also saw what I saw, but paid more attention to it than I did. At the moment it's such a fuzzy recollection I'd probably have to be hypnotized to fully recall the situations."

"That can be arranged," he said quite seriously. "Would you agree to being hypnotized?"

"Certainly. But I hope it's a last resort, and that others will have a clearer recall of the occurrences than I have had."

"How about you, Senor Winters, "did you notice anyone walking around Ted during the earring diversion? Did you see Ted sprinkle anything on his dessert?"

"Like Rhonda, I vaguely remember seeing someone up, walking around, but I paid no attention to who it might be. You might want to hypnotize me, too. I did not notice Ted putting anything on his food."

Sola turned to Carlos and asked, "What do you remember?"

"Maybe Rhonda remembered seeing me stand and thought someone moved around. I did stand and push back my chair, but I didn't move from my place at the table. I did not pass by anyone's chair, and certainly not Ted's. My attention also, was focused on finding the earring. I was looking under the chair and table and behind the chair where I was. I don't remember seeing anyone walking past my chair, but I do have a memory of movement around the table. Probably the movement was simply the acts of moving the chairs back and looking under the table. Or it could have been the maid."

Sola nodded then said, "If someone did walk past Ted's chair during the commotion, they certainly had an opportunity to sprinkle something on his food. The guests were distracted by the search, giving the killer time."

He turned to Rhonda and asked, "Do you think you could have seen someone besides Ted sprinkle something on his food? Are you sure it was Ted who did it?"

Rhonda thought a minute and said, "Honestly, I'm not sure. I'm almost positive I saw someone sprinkle something on his food, but I thought it was he. In retrospect, I remember someone saying that Ted liked coffee extra sweet, would often put three packets of sugar into it, so I thought he was making sure the dessert was sweet enough."

Rick asked, "When you knew him did he crave excessively sweet foods?"

"No. Now that you mention it, he didn't," Rhonda replied. "but I suppose people's tastes can change. I remember that when I was in college we could have all the shrimp we wanted when it was served in the cafeteria, but I wouldn't touch it. Now, I'd love to eat a bowl full of it!"

Jardín de la Unión and Valadéz Restaurant

# Chapter Fifteen

After the policeman left, Carlos suggested, "Let's walk over to the Best Western for lunch. My treat."

Rhonda grinned, "We'll take you up on that, won't we Rick? We always enjoy a free meal!"

"You bet!" Rick agreed.

They walked the few short blocks to the hotel and went into the dining room where they were seated and given menus.

"What will you have Rhonda?" Carlos asked after they had read the menu.

"Puntas de carne asada," Rhonda said to the waiter.

"I think I'll have a 'Puta', too," Rick said mispronouncing the name of the Spanish dish.

Both Rhonda and Carlos burst out laughing. The waiter, trying hard not to laugh, finally gave up and laughed with them.

"What did I say?" Rick asked, not knowing the cause of their amusement.

"You asked for a 'street walker,' a 'hooker', not steak," Rhonda chuckled.

He corrected his order, and they all ordered the same dish which was served with a salad, enchilada and guacamole.

As Rhonda buttered a slice of the delicious Mexican bread, she said, "I miss my kids. This is our first year without Jimmy."

"He's coming here for Easter, on spring break from college, so we'll see him soon," said Rick. "I wish Nikki and Juan were coming too."

"We may need for Nikki and Juan to come before this Ted-problem is over!" Rhonda exclaimed. She turned to Carlos and asked, "Haven't we told you Juan is a homicide detective in San Antonio, Texas?"

"Yes, and you have a point there," said Carlos. "I wonder if he could do some investigating there into Ginger and Ted's lives?"

"I'll bet he could!" exclaimed Rhonda. "What a good idea! Don't you think so, Rick? Especially if the police consider me a suspect."

"We'll call them tonight and discuss the problem with them, and see what he says," Rick replied.

"All of us may be considered suspects," murmured Carlos.

"Let's don't talk about it while we're eating. We need to talk about something pleasant," said Rhonda. "But when we get home let's get some paper and list the names of all the dinner guests along with possible motives.

After a pleasant and delicious lunch topped off by a sinfully fattening dessert, Carlos said, "We really ought to walk to Pipila then go down the steps embedded in the mountainside to al centro, downtown. We need the exercise."

"We do," Rick agreed, "but it's so hot."

"Just count your blessings," advised Rhonda. "Aunt Victoria phoned yesterday and said they have six inches of snow in Kansas City!"

They did decide to climb down the mountain and walk to the supermarket. After picking up a few groceries, they were thirsty, so they walked to Valadez for a coke. Several Mariachis were singing to some tourists in the restaurant, and they enjoyed listening to the music, too.

"I love this place! It's so cheerful to sit in the garden and listen to the mariachis," said Rhonda. "I wish I had hired them to sing and play at our party. Next time we have one, I may prepare American tacos and hire the Mariachis."

"Don't forget to invite me. I love your tacos!" said Carlos.

After finishing their coke, they sat in the Jardin awhile, then took a taxi back home.

After walking the dog, they settled down in the courtyard with a pad of paper and a pen with the intention of discussing motives for killing Ted.

"What do we really know about these people at the dinner party?" asked Rick. "We've only known them a couple or three months."

Rhonda remarked, "Someone at that dinner is dangerous. Carlos, would you help us put heavy chains across the doors? I'm not going to let anyone who went to that dinner inside this house!"

"Of course," he agreed. "That's actually a wise idea. We'll use chains like I use in my townhouse in Mexico City."

"I don't know about chains. What if we had a fire? We might have trouble getting out," Rick objected.

"What's to burn?" asked Carlos. "There's no wood in this house. It's all brick, rock, concrete, tile and wrought iron."

"You're right," Rick agreed. "I forget I'm not back in Kansas City in my wooden house. Now let's get to the subject of motives."

Each person began suggesting motives, so Rhonda wrote on the paper:
12 Suspects

Reasons why Ted might have been killed:
1. Blackmailing person about a secret.
2. For an inheritance
3. Revenge
4. Because he is a danger to society
I. Motives: Did Ted know someone's secret? Was the secret:
   1. Alcoholism?
   2. Drugs?

3. Abortion?
4. Embezzlement?
5. Police record?
6. Mental illness?
7. Secret love affair?
8. Illegitimate child?
9. Blackmail? Bribery?
10. Bigamy?
11. Attempted rape of child or relative?
12. Former work as stripper or prostitute?
13. Involved in Mafia? Organized crime?

II Money
1. Does Ted have a will? Who is the beneficiary?
2. Does he really have a fortune in Switzerland?
3. Royalties form his poetry and songs?
4. Won lottery? Inheritance? Life insurance policy?

III Revenge.

As far as we know he had only beaten his two wives and frittered away their money. Both may have considered this the first opportunity to get revenge. However, there may be another person present who Ted had cheated or hurt in some way.

IV. Danger to society

Who would know this better than Ginger and Dr. Gomez? Let's use our imaginations and brainstorm some more," Rick said. "How would the killer know exactly how much poison to give Ted? How would he know the amount which constitutes a legal dose?"

"Wouldn't a doctor, a pharmacist or a nurse know about arsenic and how much would kill? Aren't there books in the library that would contain this information?" asked Rhonda.

"Perhaps one of the dinner guests has worked for a pharmacist and has knowledge of drugs, herbs and poisons,"

Carlos suggested.

Rhonda said, "Marta Gomez grows herbs in her home for medicinal purposes. She showed her herb garden to me one day when I was there."

"I can think of four people with access to that information," said Carlos. "They are: Dr. Gomez, Marta Gomez, Ginger and I. I have access since my uncle is a doctor."

Ignoring his comment, Rhonda said, "Perhaps the poison was only meant to make Ted sick or to scare him, not kill him. Perhaps Ted was blackmailing someone, and the poison was meant only as a warning to him. None of us know these people well enough to know if they have some deep, dark secret they want to hide. Perhaps Ted inadvertently stumbled upon their secret and threatened them with blackmail?"

"Do you think Ted was capable of blackmail?" Rick asked.

"Absolutely!" exclaimed Rhonda.

Rick said, "In the Agatha Christie novels the crime is usually committed by the least likely suspect. Who do you think are the least likely suspects in this crime?"

"The three of us!" Rhonda exclaimed. "And Professor Almire," she added as an afterthought. "I am 100% sure the three of us are innocent and 95% sure about the professor."

"How do you know the professor doesn't have a deep, dark secret that he would kill to protect?" asked Rick. "You only knew him for six weeks, and that was 35 years ago."

"True," grinned Rhonda. "I guess I'm only sure about one person, and that's me!"

"Who are the other least likely suspects?" Rick asked.

"Probably the minister, his wife, and the Sunday School teacher. In your opinion, anyway," replied Carlos, grinning.

"Murderers can be pleasant, seemingly normal people," Rhonda interjected. "Often on the news we hear neighbors of a convicted murderer exclaiming how shocked they were. They would say that he was such a nice person, always helpful and friendly, and that this action was unbelievable."

Rick said, "Let's mention each person's name who was a dinner guest and try to think of possible reasons why someone might hate Ted or consider him a threat. Let's start with Felipe."

Rhonda said, "Perhaps he is a very jealous man, and he has noticed Ted trying to flirt with Anita."

"Felipe sat too far away from Ted to have poisoned his food," Carlos pointed out.

"Unless he had gotten up walked past Ted's chair and sprinkled the arsenic on his food while everyone's attention was on finding Marta's earring," said Rhonda. She added, "What if Marta dropped her earring on purpose to create a diversion so that someone she was in cahoots with could tamper with Ted's food? What if she had a secret lover and Ted threatened to tell his wife? What if Felipe was her lover?"

"Rhonda, we're getting too far afield with such suppositions," Rick reprimanded her.

"I thought we were supposed to use our imaginations," she replied. "Besides you never know. Preacher and doctor or not, people are much  the same the world over, rich or poor, educated or uneducated.  They all have the same basic instincts."

"Do they?" Rick asked.

"Maybe everyone except you," she retorted.

Carlos glanced quickly at Rhonda, but said nothing.

Rick ignored her comment and said, "Now let's talk about Suspect number 2--Anita. Perhaps Anita is afraid of Ted and suspects he has a mental problem. She is worried that he is a danger in her home."

Carlos added, "She sat next to him, and had opportunity.

She cooked much of the dinner, but I can see no conceivable way that she could have poisoned only the portion that Ted ate, because she didn't serve it to him."

"Perhaps she filled a 'special' plate for him and instructed the maid to serve it only to Ted?" Rhonda suggested. "But that would be risky. The maid could serve it to the wrong person, and also when questioned by the police she might confess what she did. Also, maybe the food was meant for Ginger, but the maid gave it to Ted by mistake."

"Why would Anita want to hurt Ginger?" Rick asked, curiously.

"Because she was jealous of her. You've got to admit Ginger is a pretty woman. Perhaps she thought Ginger was flirting with Felipe. Maybe she caught her kissing him."

"But Anita is also attractive. A little overweight, but attractive," Rick said. "She has beautiful brown eyes, her hair is always nicely styled and she is stylishly dressed!"

"My, you've certainly been looking her over, haven't you?" Rhonda teased.

Carlos said, "Perhaps Anita had only pretended to dislike Ted. Had she thrown herself at him and been rejected? 'Hell hath no fury like a woman scorned', they say."

Rhonda laughed. "That's a good one! Who knows? It could be true."

"Let's talk about Juanita now," Rick suggested. "What do we know about her? She is a widow, has one daughter who is in college. She's our Sunday School teacher, and a good one. She is also an attractive lady, short dark hair with a little grey creeping in."

"She has a beautiful figure," Rhonda said. "I'm envious, so I'll make up a bad story about her. Let's say she was born poor, but smart and ambitious. She worked her way through college as a stripper in Laredo. Perhaps Ted had seen her dance, remembered her and told her where he had seen her. Worried that he would tell the others, she poisoned his food during the commotion over Marta's earring."

"I can't think of a thing to add to that," laughed Carlos.

"Then how about Professor Almire?" asked Rick. "Perhaps Ted had borrowed money from him and wouldn't pay him back? That's not a bad enough motive, however. Let's say Ted tried to rape his daughter or granddaughter?"

"Ted wouldn't have done that," said Rhonda.

"You keep telling me that I don't know what a person might do. People will surprise you, you tell me."

She laughed. "Who knows his true character? Ted probably was far worse than I would have thought. But the professor would never have jeopardized his reputation and standing in the community by committing murder. He would have gone through the proper channels of turning him over to the police."

"Do you agree with Rhonda's assertion of his character, Carlos? You knew him."

"Yes," agreed Carlos. "He is a fine, upstanding man."

"Let's talk about Dr. Gomez, then," suggested Rick. "Do you know anything about him, Carlos?"

"He's another fine man. I'd be surprised to hear anything bad about him. Since they are both in the medical profession, I phoned my Uncle Guillermo yesterday and asked him about Gomez. He had never heard a whisper of any rumor or scandal about him. Of course, there's always the chance he has had a secret affair with one of his patients. Sometimes patients fall in love with their doctors and vice versa. He could have given the wrong medicine to one of his patients. People make mistakes. He could have felt that Ted was a danger to society and done society a favor. Perhaps Ginger did phone him and they were very close, then Ted caught them together."

"How about Dr. Marta Gomez?" Rick asked, moving the discussion along.

"I've never heard a word against her and neither had my uncle. So she grows herbs and knows about their medicinal qualities. Big deal! Arsenic doesn't grow in the garden! She probably only saw Ted twice. Once at your home and once at the Lopez's dinner."

"She's a cute woman, I think," Rhonda said, "Petite and cute. Her short, bleached blonde hair looks good on her. She could also have some secret that Ted learned about." she yawned. "Who knows? I'm getting tired of this game."

"Let's talk about one more. Ginger. She's the most likely suspect. Most people would guess the wife first. Probably the police have been checking her out, and questioning her until she's ready to scream."

"She seemed to worship the ground he walked on," Rhonda remarked.

"Now Rhonda, think for a minute about your marriage to Ted," said Carlos. "No matter how much you might have cared for him when you married him didn't your affection for him die an early death after all of the abuse he dished out? Ginger has only been married to him for year, but isn't that about how long your marriage to him lasted?"

"Now that you mention it," she said, "I agree that Ginger may have been fed up with him. But divorce is infinitely easier than murder."

"Then again," Rick interrupted, "there's always the chance that Ted committed suicide."

Carlos turned to Rhonda, "When you knew him would you have considered him to be suicidal. Did he ever mention suicide to you?"

"Only once," she replied, "And I'm certain he wasn't serious then."

"What was the circumstance?" asked Carlos.

"He was angry with me one evening and he cut both of my arms with a broken glass. When the blood continued to gush out, he reluctantly took me to the emergency room of a nearby hospital where I had twelve stitches in my left arm and two in my right one. Naturally I was extremely angry about it and we had a big fight about it sometime later. He hit me again, and I got away, ran outside and on to a store where I called my mother and step-dad from a pay phone. They came to pick me up, and when I went back into the apartment to pack, he yelled, "If you leave me I will kill myself!"

As I went out the door I retorted, "Do it in the basement so I won't have such a mess to clean up!"

Rick observed dryly, "Obviously he had not been serious."

Carlos murmured, "Unfortunately."

"But why would anyone kill for those reasons on our list?" asked Rick. "They could simply say that they were young when they made that mistake and thankful they now had the sense never to repeat it. Of course any of those "secrets" we listed would be embarrassing and humiliating. They would be ashamed for others to know, but they wouldn't kill because of them. Would they?"

"You might not," said Rhonda loyally, knowing what a good man Rick is, "but some people would."

"I agree," said Carlos. "For example, if the Baptist preacher had had an illicit love affair and an illegitimate child since he has been married and Ted knew about it he might kill Ted to keep him from telling his wife. If that knowledge were spread to Anita and to his congregation he would probably lose both his wife and his job."

Rhonda said, "I could be accused of killing him for revenge. To get even with him for beating me, for his mental and physical cruelty to me."

"You're off the hook," laughed Rick.

"Why?" Rhonda asked.

"You don't know a thing about arsenic."

"How do you know? Maybe I do. Do any of us really know another person?" Rhonda asked. "At one time I really hated Ted. When I threatened to divorce him, he would tell me that I could be forced to pay him alimony if I did. We were separated about two years before I filed for divorce. Remember Carlos, when you visited me in Kansas City and found out I was married, but separated. You were so angry that I hadn't told you that I'd been married, you left without saying goodbye."

"I remember that only too well. Ted certainly messed things up for me," muttered Carlos.

"He messed things up for me, too. But after you left I learned Ted was living in another town, so I filed for divorce and he never knew he was divorced until months after it was final."

"How did you manage that?" asked Rick.

"My attorney said I could keep the divorce secret from him if I would put an ad in a legal paper every week for six weeks, stating that I was filing for divorce, and if Ted didn't contest it, I could be legally divorced without informing him. Of course, he would never see the ad in a legal newspaper, therefore he couldn't contest it if he didn't know about it."

Carlos shook his head. "Rhonda you were always tricky. Did you ever inform him he was a free man?"

"About three months after we were divorced, I wrote and told him. He replied to my letter and told me he really had loved me."

"Strange kind of love considering he beat you on a regular basis," Rick retorted.

"True," Rhonda agreed.

"Do you think you were ever legally divorced?" Carlos asked.

The lawyer said it was legal, so I certainly hope so! If not, Ted, Rick and I are bigamists!" Rhonda laughed.

"No," said Carlos. "Not anymore you aren't!"

"Oh oh! Rick, now you have a motive for murder!" Rhonda remarked, grinning wickedly.

"And I have a motive," said Carlos, "because Ted messed up everything for me."

"That was only a temporary upset for you," said Rhonda, "and you were over it thirty years ago. I'm afraid that won't be considered a motive."

"Why do you say it was a temporary upset?" he asked.

Because when I came to Mexico after my divorce, as a free woman, to see you, you dumped me! You certainly got over it fast!"

"Did I?" he asked solemnly.

# Chapter Sixteen

"Carlos, why don't we conduct our own investigation like we did last summer?" Rhonda asked at dinner that evening, as they were eating Chicken Tetrazzini and strawberry jello salad.

"Good idea!" he agreed. "Don't you think so, Rick?"

"I do," he said.

"Let's send our maid to take cookies to Anita and Felipe with instructions that she must make an opportunity to be alone with their maid. What's her name? Alejandra, I believe."

"Why not?" Rick agreed. "Wasn't that the strategy you two used last summer with good success? I understand it worked out well."

The next day when Camila came to work, Rhonda asked her, as Carlos interpreted, if she would take some cookies to the Lopez home.

When she agreed, Rhonda asked if she would do some detective work while she was there.

This caused Camila to laugh delightedly, "Like Mata Hari?" she asked.

Rhonda nodded, grinning, while Carlos explained to her that her assignment was to arrange a private chat with their maid, Alejandra, and try to learn anything she could pertaining to Ted's murder.

When Camila returned she told them, with Carlos translating, that Alejandra was not really a maid. She was Felipe's niece, who was hired to help out while the Saxons were visiting. Apparently, Ted, who thought she was a maid, had harassed her, trying several times to kiss her. The day of the dinner party Ted had come behind her while she was trying to make the bed in his room and had tried to push her down on the bed. She had screamed and Felipe rushed in and grabbed Ted. He told Ted to pack his bags and get out. Anita walked in as all of this was going on and said since he and Ginger were leaving the next day and the dinner party was scheduled for that evening they would forgive Ted if he promised never to touch Alejandra again. She said he promised and apologized profusely.

Carlos turned to Rhonda and asked, since Camila did not understand English, "Did he have a roving eye when you were married to him?"

"Not that I was ever aware of, but that doesn't mean he didn't when my back was turned. 'Leopards can't change their spots anymore than skunks can change the stripes on their backs,' but who knows?"

"It's doubtful that Ginger knew he was playing around, either," Rick commented.

Carlos turned back to Camila. "You did a good job to learn that from Alejandra, she must like to talk."

"I think that girl would tell everything she knows," grinned Camila. "She's young and hasn't learned to hold her tongue, so I took advantage of that fact and kept quizzing her. Luckily she was home alone, so she felt free to talk. She said she had helped prepare dinner, had served the food, picked up the plates after each course was eaten, refilled drinks, cut the dessert into squares, then served it.

She said she was worried that she would be considered a suspect, that she had not liked Ted, but she certainly would not have killed him."

"Sounds like a case of 'the guilty flee when no man pursueth,' " Rhonda quoted.

"She did have both motive and opportunity," Rick agreed.

"I can't believe she would kill Ted for horsing around," said Rhonda. "He never tried anything like that with me before we were married."

"Never tried to kiss you?" Rick asked, surprised.

"I meant he never tried to push me onto a bed and you-know," she answered, blushing.

Carlos changed the subject by turning back to Camila, "What else did you learn, Mata Hari?"

Camila laughed and told him that she had asked Alejandra if there was any arsenic in the garage, and was told she thought there was some in the greenhouse which they used as a weed killer."

"I wonder if the police have learned about that?" Rick inquired.

Before anyone could comment, Camila added that she had learned a little about Alejandra's background. She's Felipe's brother's daughter, and she lives with her parents, walking distance from Felipe's home. Her last name is also Lopez, obviously. She's twenty one years old, and a college student at the University of Guanajuato, a business major. She said she was glad to earn some extra money working for her aunt and uncle. She has a boyfriend, but it's not serious. They're just friends. She's a pretty girl, isn't she?"

Carlos asked her, "Camila, did you ask her any questions about Ted and Ginger?"

"She said neither Felipe nor Anita liked Ted because he was so argumentative. On one occasion he accused Alejandra of stealing pesos out of his billfold. She was very indignant about that.

Alejandra also said she frequently heard Ted fussing with Ginger and saw him slap her face once. She said he was really strange. Once when she came to clean house, she was wearing a red dress and he told her he thought she was a devil because the devil wore red. She also said his behavior was excessive. Sometimes he would drink a dozen bottles of Coke. They had to hide the Coke because he would drink all there was and never offer to buy any or replenish the supply. He would take several showers daily. She said, she counted seven damp towels one day. At least he was clean in his personal habits. She said he also slept excessively. Some days he laid in bed all day, only getting up to eat."

Carlos complimented Camila on her sleuthing, then asked her, "Do you, by any chance, know the Gomez's maid?"

"Certainly!" she said grinning, "As a matter of fact, I know Elisa quite well."

"Great!" he exclaimed. "How would you like to visit her soon?"

# Chapter Seventeen

After lunch, Rick phoned their daughter and son-in-law, a homicide detective who lived in San Antonio, Texas, to tell them about the predicament of the reappearance and subsequent murder of Rhonda's ex-husband.

"I'm worried that because Rhonda made the cake which the poison was probably sprinkled over that she will be considered a suspect in this case. If she ends up in jail we'll never get her out!"

Nikki laughed, "I can just see Mom in a black and white striped jailbird suit!"

"It's not a laughing matter, Nikki. This is serious. I want to talk to Juan."

She put her husband, Juan, on the phone. Rick reiterated to him what he had just told Nikki. "Juan, I want you to do me a favor," he said. "Can you pull some strings and get me as much information as possible about Ted Saxon and Ginger Rhodes Saxon? Ted's full name is Theodore Lyndon Saxon. Apparently, she was a psychiatric nurse at a state mental hospital and Ted was a patient there, diagnosed with paranoid schizophrenia. He was probably there last year, and maybe part of this year. Are you writing this down?"

"Yes, I think I have everything. Do you spell Saxon S-A-X-O-N? And Rhodes R-H-O-D-E-S?" Juan asked.

"That's right. Now Juan, this is very important because there's a killer loose here in our crowd, and none of us feel very safe, to put it mildly. Can you find out about both Ted and Ginger's backgrounds, Ted's hospitalization, his diagnosis, her employment, jail records for either of them, any pertinent information? This is serious and we need the information as soon as possible."

"That's a tall order! But fortunately today is my day off work, and the person who can get those records owes me a favor. I'll see what I can do and get back with you."

"Thanks a lot, son. I really appreciate this. Oh, there's one more thing. Try to find out if Ted has a will and who his beneficiary is, will you?"

"Sure. I'll be in touch. Adiós."

Rhonda was listening while he made the call. "Thanks, Rick. I appreciate your concern."

They went out to the courtyard where Carlos was sitting and Rick told him that Juan was going to try to get some information for them.

"That's good," said Carlos. "I hope he is able to find out all about them."

"I hope you two don't mind having leftovers for dinner?"

"Not if it's Chicken Tetrazzini!" Carlos exclaimed. "I love it!"

"So do I," Rick agreed. "The olives are the secret ingredient."

"There's something I want to talk to you two about," said Carlos. "You've been very kind to let me stay here so long, but I feel like I'm imposing and should move to my Uncle's home."

"First of all, you are not imposing. Is he, Rick?"

"Not at all. Stay as long as you wish," he replied.

"Secondly," continued Rhonda, "You can't move to your uncle's home. He lives in Leon, and the police said not to leave Guanajuato until the murder is solved."

"I should move to a hotel then," Carlos said.

"Oh Carlos, don't go. I feel safer having two men in the house until this murder is solved."

"I'd much prefer to stay with you if you're sure you don't mind." Carlos acquiesced. "but I'm going to the grocery store after while and stock your pantry. It's my turn to buy groceries."

"You certainly don't have to."

"I want to," he said.

"Excuse me, guys," said Rhonda. "I'm going to mix up some brownies."

"I hope you're going to make the ones with the chocolate mint pattie frosting," Carlos said. "My, are those delicious!"

"I'm almost afraid to make something you suggest," Rhonda laughed. "Remember what happened last time!"

"What happened?" Rick asked.

"Didn't I tell you that it was Carlos' brilliant suggestion that I make that Four Layered Chocolate Dessert aptly named Death by Chocolate to take to Felipe and Anita's dinner party? It will be my luck to end up in jail because of it, too!"

Rick burst out laughing. "Carlos, I hope you can help her break out of jail."

"If I go, he's going with me! I'll tell them he made me do it!"

Carlos said, "I do feel badly about that. I'm going to phone Agente Rivera tomorrow and see if he can help us get out of this jam."

"Not a bad idea, but first let's wait and see if we need him. Hopefully the Guanajuato police will find the killer without implicating me," she said before she went into the kitchen.

They had just finished eating dinner when the phone rang. Rhonda answered and Rick got on an extension when he learned it was Juan.

Apparently Nikki was on the extension at their apartment because she said, "Hi Mom and Dad. Has Juan got news for you!"

"You sound cheerful. I hope it's good news," said Rhonda.

"Let's put it this way," replied her daughter, "it's interesting news!"

"We have a copy here of Ted's will," Juan began. "It was dated June 6, 1964 and you'll never guess who his heir is!"

"Oh no!" groaned Rhonda. "I'm in big trouble if it's me!"

"Then you're in big trouble, Mom!" laughed Nikki. "You're his sole beneficiary."

"Nikki, you don't seem to realize the seriousness of this problem. Your Mom could be thrown in jail and tried for murder," Rick reprimanded her. "She's in trouble if the police here get a copy of that record. I wish you could suppress the evidence."

"I'm sorry, Mom. You know we'll do everything we can to help you. I'm laughing because of the letter to you included in the will. Do you want to hear it?"

"Yes. Go ahead."

"It says, "Hi Bubbles!

I always promised to buy you a mink coat. Take the royalties from the songs I have sold and buy the coat of your choice. I hope there's enough for a full length one. Never let it be said that Ted Saxon welched on a promise! If there's any money left keep it for my half of the rent, utilities and groceries which I never paid you.

If my poems are ever published the proceeds from them are also yours.

Sorry about that secret Swiss bank account. That was just a figment of my fertile imagination, told just to impress you!

Think of me when you wear that mink coat, Bubbles!

Love,
Ted"

Nikki burst out laughing again. "Bubbles!" teased Nikki.

Rick said, "Thank you, Juan. We really appreciate it. Keep a copy of the will in your safe deposit box, but don't send it to Mexico. We're going to play dumb like we don't know anything about this, because when the police here find out about it, your mom is in trouble. They will believe this was her motive for killing him."

"Mom, I'm sorry," Nikki said contritely.

Juan said, "I should have more information for you tomorrow or the next day. I did learn one thing about Ginger. She wasn't working as a psychiatric nurse when Ted was in the mental hospital. The office was closing and the computer was shut down so that's all I know for now, but I should be able to get a full report in the morning. Talk to you tomorrow."

Anita phoned Rhonda that evening and said, "I'm at a store near my house calling you from a pay phone. I think you should know that Ginger got a copy of Ted's will faxed to her at Felipe's office, and you are Ted's sole beneficiary. She is furious, to say the least."


### Layered Strawberry Salad

| | |
|---|---|
| 6 oz pkg strawberry jello | 1 large can crushed |
| 2 cups boiling water |    pineapple, drained |
| 1 large box frozen strawberries | 2-3 sliced bananas |
| | 12 ounces sour cream |

Dissolve jello in boiling water. Add strawberries, pineapple and bananas. Pour 1/2 mixture into bottom of 9x13 inch dish. Chill until firm (or put in freezer 15-20 minutes). Remove from freezer and spread with sour cream and pour remaining jello mixture over all. Refrigerate until set.

# Chicken Tetrazzini

2 cups chopped celery
1 1/2 cups chopped onion
3 tablespoons butter or margarine
2 cups chicken broth
1 tablespoon Worcestershire
   sauce
Salt and pepper
1 cup chopped pecans
1 (101/2 oz) can condensed
   cream of mushroom soup

1/2 cup milk
1 cup grated sharp cheese
1/2 pound spaghetti,
   cooked and drained
6 cups chopped, cooked
   chicken
1/2 cup sliced stuffed
   olives

In a saucepan, cook celery and onion in butter until tender. Add chicken broth, Worcestershire sauce, salt, and pepper. Simmer about 15 minutes. Slowly stir in mushroom soup, milk, and cheese. Mix thoroughly. Remove from heat. Add cooked spaghetti. Let stand for 1 hour. Preheat oven to 350 degrees. Grease a 9x13 inch baking dish. Add chicken and olives to spaghetti. Place in prepared dish. Sprinkle with chopped pecans. Bake 20 to 25 minutes or until hot and bubbly. Makes 12 servings.

## Brownies with Mint Frosting

1 pkg. Pillsbury fudge
   brownie mix

1 (16 oz) pkg Brach's
   chocolate covered mint
   patties

Prepare and bake brownie mix as package directs, baking in a greased 9x13 inch pan. Remove from heat. Unwrap and place chocolate mints in rows over brownies. Return to oven for about 5 minutes or until chocolate has melted. Take spatula and spread chocolate over brownies. Cool. Cut into squares. Serves 20.

# Chapter Eighteen

Suspicion fell, at first, on Ginger because it was thought that she would inherit and benefit financially at Ted's death. But when it was discovered that Rhonda was his sole beneficiary, the police believed she had both motive and opportunity.

Rhonda assumed Ginger had told the police that she was Ted's first wife and had convinced them that she had hated him and had poisoned him by sprinkling arsenic over his dessert, when everyone's attention was on finding Marta's earring.

When the police came to her home with a search warrant, she was shocked even though she had realized it could happen. Rick wasn't home, but Carlos stood by her side to translate.

"Surely I am not a suspect?" she questioned the officer.

"We have to suspect everyone until they are proved innocent," he replied. "This is just routine."

"May I ask why you are going to search my house?"

"We were informed that Senor Saxon, had beaten you in the past and that you're still holding a grudge against him."

"Do you honestly think I'd hold a grudge for 35 years?" she asked, astonished.

"I don't know. Some people hold grudges for longer than that," he told her.

"Well, I don't-- for a very good reason. I used to resent it when people wronged me, but after I discovered that I had cancer and learned that anger, stress, and holding grudges had contributed to this disease, I changed my ways. Now when I become angry I say to myself, "you can't afford the luxury of that negative thought," then I switch my mind to a pleasant thought. I can truly tell you that I don't hate anyone."

"That's good advice for everyone," he said. "Is your cancer in remission?"

"Yes, it has been for over six years."

Carlos asked them, "Who signed the search warrant? Was it commandante Javier Valdez?"

"No," the policeman replied. "he is out of town and has been for two days. He should be back tomorrow."

"Tell him to call Señora Winters as soon as he returns," Carlos ordered.

"Si Señor." the policeman replied, then turned his attention to Rhonda. "We do have a search warrant, Señora. May we begin?"

"Go right ahead and search the house. I have nothing to hide," she replied. "But first I want to ask you a question. I assume you wouldn't be here if someone had not accused me of this crime. Was Ginger Saxon my accuser? She's the only one who knew that Ted beat me."

"I'm sorry, but I'm not at liberty to answer that question," he replied.

Rick returned home about the time the search began. He was speechless as they searched all the rooms and closets downstairs. They found nothing, then they went upstairs to the office. First they searched the file cabinets and the book shelves thoroughly flipping through each book. Then they searched all of the desk drawers, finding nothing except one sealed envelope.

"We need to open this envelope," said the agente who had brought it downstairs to show her.

"Certainly," Rhonda agreed, then she took a second look at the envelope. "Funny. I don't remember ever seeing a sealed envelope in my desk. When you open it I would also like to see what's inside it."

He opened it in front of her and took out a single sugar

packet. Wearing gloves and treating the envelope and packet as evidence, he noted that the packet had been opened and did contain something white. "This will have to be analyzed so we will know whether or not it contains sugar."

The thought that she had been framed suddenly filled Rhonda with dread, fear and tension. How could she prove that she had not put the envelope or the packet in her desk? How could she prove her innocence, she wondered.

Rick told the police that the envelope could have been put there by numerous people. He said they had had two parties in the house in the past month or so, and most of the guests had toured the house and had been inside the office.

The policeman suggested she might prepare a list of all the people who had been inside her home since the Saxons came to Guanajuato.

Rhonda thought a minute then said, "I can only think of one person who has been alone in my office, and that was Ginger. I left her there alone so she could make a private phone call."

Rick, concerned about the situation, said, "You can rest assured that she is the culprit who hid the packet in the desk. Where did you find it? Was it in the front of the desk where it could be easily seen or was it hidden under some papers?"

"It was definitely hidden under papers, placed in the back of the desk in the middle drawer. There was no writing on the sealed envelope. It will, of course, be tested for fingerprints, as will the packet."

"I'm going to phone Ginger and ask her about it," Rhonda declared.

"We would prefer that you do not," said the policeman. "Let us handle it."

"I'm sure she put it there," Rhonda grumbled after the police had left.

"I'm sure she did, too," said Carlos. "Jealousy would be her motive. She's jealous of you because you were her husband's former wife."

"Why would she be jealous of me? I certainly was not interested in Ted. I wouldn't have him if he had a million dollar bill wrapped around him! She's welcome to him!"

"Ann Landers would probably tell you that the wife is usually jealous of her husband's former wife," Rick said, grinning.

"Maybe so, but you can imagine the former wife is only thankful to the new wife for taking him off her hands!" she laughed. "Actually, I don't know why I should be laughing. Now that the sugar packet was found in my desk, I will be considered a prime suspect."

"Not if there's sugar in the packet," Carlos said.

"There won't be sugar in the packet," Rhonda mumbled. "Ginger wouldn't have put the packet there if it contained sugar. They will find arsenic. And the $24,000 question is: Where did she get the arsenic?"

The fact that she put it in your desk two or three weeks ago implies premeditation," said Rick. "That is, if she was the one who put it there. Unfortunately many other people have also been in there."

"Who else would have done it?" Rhonda asked resignedly.

"Are you angry, Rhonda?" asked Carlos.

"Of course I'm angry! Why would you even ask me such a question? Can't you tell I'm angry?"

"Yes, I can, and I'm noticing that you aren't practicing what you preach. I want you to take a deep breathe right now."

"Why?"

"Just take a deep breathe and let it out slowly," he said, grinning. "Then repeat after me, "I can't afford the luxury of these negative thoughts!"

# Chapter Nineteen

Commandante Javier Valdez phoned Rhonda the following morning and apologized about being out of town when her house was searched. "There was nothing I could have done about it, I don't suppose," he grumbled. "I was glad I had not been asked to sign the warrant, however."

"Has the envelope been tested for fingerprints? Was sugar found in the packet?" she asked.

"The envelope and packet have been tested but there were no fingerprints on either, which indicates to me that you did not put it there. Unfortunately, arsenic mixed with sugar was in the packet."

"Oh no! I'm being framed! I hope you know that."

"Yes, I believe you have been," he said. "There's nothing I can do about it at the moment, but you may rest assured I'll do my best to help you."

"Thank you, Javier. I appreciate that," she said, then changed the subject and asked, "Can't the Guanajuato police get information about Ted and Ginger's backgrounds from the States?"

"If a person doesn't have a criminal record, there's little that can be found. The police stations have only official records about people such as arrests, lawsuits and possibly military records. However, we can dig up everything we need to know about a person if he or she is a strong suspect."

"There's always a chance that Ted had a criminal record. I've heard that many schizophrenics do. And as for Ginger, isn't a wife (not an ex-wife) usually a prime suspect if her husband is murdered?"

"At this time she is not considered a strong suspect.

Therefore I can't do much digging."

"All right," she murmured bitterly.

"Rhonda, don't worry about this packet. It has obviously been planted. You have more sense than to have placed such an envelope in your desk. Even I have been in your office, as have many others. We are aware of that. I must go now, but don't worry."

"That's easy for you to say," she thought to herself but said only, "Thank you for calling. Adiós."

Carlos came into the living room and she told him they had found arsenic in the packet. He didn't reply, just asked, "May I use the phone now?"

"Certainly."

He took a phone number out of his billfold and dialed. "May I speak to Agente Rivera?" he asked. "This is Carlos Selva, and it's important that I talk to him."

While he was waiting for Rivera to come to the phone he said to Rhonda, "Don't worry. Rivera will help you. I'm sure of it."

Carlos was worried since he learned about the arsenic. He and Rhonda had met Agente Rivera the previous summer when they were in San Miguel de Allende, a town about an hour away from Guanajuato. While in San Miguel on business, they had inadvertently gotten mixed up in a murder there. They had worked with the detective in an effort to prove their innocence and had helped solve the case.

When Agente Rivera came on the phone, Carlos explained that he and Rhonda were in trouble again, and told him what had happened.

"We need your help, please," Carlos told him. "Would you phone the Commandante Javier Valdez in Guanajuato and tell him what you know about Rhonda? She could use a good recommendation from you."

"You will? Thanks," said Carlos. "By the way, do you know Agente Sola here? If so, I'd really appreciate it if you'd talk to him also, and vouch for Rhonda."

After Carlos got off the phone, Rhonda hugged him. "You're a great friend, Carlos. I feel better already."

"Bueno!" he said, smiling at her. "Now, we've got to get the Maid Network going. What time does Camila come today?"

"She had a doctor's appointment this morning, so she won't be here until 1:00."

"Hopefully at 1:00 nobody will be home except the Gomez's maid. In case they are home, do you have some cookies you can send over, which will give Camila an excuse for going there?"

"Sure. I'll go to the kitchen and put a couple of dozen in a container."

When Camila arrived she was sent on her way to the Gomez home to pump their maid.

Rhonda felt like throwing herself onto her bed and having a good cry, but just then Rick returned home from the video store and she told him about Javier's call, about Carlos' talk with the San Miguel detective, and that Camila had been sent to spy on the Gomez family.

"At least you're staying busy," he said, "And that's good."

"Too busy to prepare a very good lunch," she said just as the phone rang.

She answered it, yelled at Rick that it was Nikki and to get on the other line.

"Hi darling," she said to her daughter. "Do you have some juicy information for us?"

"Afraid not, Mom. The man who was getting the scoop for Juan had a slight heart attack and he's in the hospital."

"Oh no! Do they expect him to be OK?"

"Sure, but he might not return to work for a week or more."

"Well, that's a bummer," Rhonda complained. "It seems like life is two steps foreward and two steps backwards."

"Juan will get the information as soon as he can," Nikki assured her Mom.

"I hope it won't be too late," she groaned. "Our house was searched by the cops and they found arsenic in my desk. Someone planted it there, and I think it was Ginger. Can't he get the information from anyone else?"

"No, but we have a vacation before long. Maybe we can come down and help you catch the killer."

"Just say when and we'll send you some airline tickets," Rick said. "I'm very worried."

After she hung up Rhonda prepared grilled cheese sandwiches and tomato soup for lunch.

"The soup is good," Carlos complimented her. "How did you fix it?"

"Opened a can and heated it," she grinned. "It's a one-ingredient recipe."

# Chapter Twenty

Rhonda arrived early at the University, about thirty minutes before she was to start teaching her class, so that she could talk to Anita.

She found Anita in her classroom, sitting at her desk, grading papers. "Hi," she said. "It's my turn to buy your lunch. Are you free today after class?"

"Sure," Anita said smiling. "How are you?"

"Ok, I guess. My, we've all had a time, haven't we?" groaned Rhonda.

"And it's all my fault. If I hadn't insisted on having that farewell dinner party, none of this would have happened. I could kick myself for not listening to you, Rhonda. You told me I shouldn't have the party."

"Don't blame yourself, Anita. It probably would have happened anyway. Just somewhere else or at a different time."

The students began to arrive, so Rhonda prepared to leave. "I'll meet you here later, Anita, if that's OK."

After their classes were over, they walked to the Posada de Santa Fe where they ate lunch. Afterwards, they sat on a bench in the jardin and talked for about an hour.

"Anita, I appreciate your phone call about Ted's will. Apparently he forgot to change it after he re-married. Ginger must have been aware that he had a will. How else could she have gotten a copy of it so soon?"

"I don't know, but she was really angry after she read it," Anita remarked.

"Frankly I doubt he had enough that it's worth squabbling over. Tell her all I want is the $2,000 I feel he owed me. If there's anything left, she's welcome to it."

"Do you really want me to tell her that?"

"Certainly. Then maybe she'll get over her mad spell," Rhonda replied.

"She is really acting odd. I guess it's her way of grieving," Anita said.

"Do you mind still having her at your house?"

"Frankly, I'll be glad when she's gone," Anita confided to Rhonda. "It will be nice when Felipe and I can have our home all to ourselves again. I guess she can't go until the case is solved, though."

"Have the police been pestering you?" Rhonda asked.

"I'll say!" she exclaimed. "They've been here several times to question each of us. It's embarrassing! The neighbors probably think we're like those sisters in the book, <u>Arsenic and Old Lace</u>!"

Rhonda laughed. "I don't know why I'm laughing. It's not funny. I can't believe anyone at your dinner would have killed Ted. Therefore, the only conclusion I can come to is that he must have killed himself."

"Felipe and I have discussed that, and we think it is a distinct possibility. Ginger said she thinks he had been slowly poisoning himself over the past few weeks. She didn't think he knew that poisoning would be a painful death. She thought he believed the poison would simply cause his heart to stop beating and he would fall asleep and not wake up. He had read a book where a poison had been added to someone's champagne, and that person died almost immediately."

"That must have been what happened. Suicide is the only solution that makes sense in this case." Rhonda paused a minute, then asked, "Did you ever see Ted sprinkle sugar over his food from a small paper packet?'

"I've seen him add sugar from packets to his coffee," she said. "He carried those sugar packets in his pocket."

"Isn't that strange? I wonder why he didn't use your sugar? You always served sugar and cream with coffee."

"I can only think of two reasons why he didn't. Mexican sugar isn't as finely granulated as that he was used to in the states. He either preferred the fine sugar grains in the packets or else he had mixed poison with the sugar and used this method to slowly poison himself."

"Have you discussed this theory with the police?" Rhonda asked.

"We did, and they duly jotted the information into a notebook, but I guess they have to check out all other leads and if everyone has an alibi, then they may look more carefully at the possibility of suicide."

"Let's change the subject," Rhonda suggested. "Do you know the Gomez Family very well?"

"Not really. They are both respected doctors. I heard someone say once that Guanajuato was fortunate to have doctors here of their caliber."

"Have they always lived in Guanajuato?"

"No. They've only been here for four or five years. I think they have a married daughter in some nearby town. Irapuato, I believe. And a grandson, I heard."

"They seem very nice," said Rhonda. "I like them a lot."

"That's why I invited them," Anita began, answering Rhonda's unasked question. "I had noticed that they were at your party, so I assumed you liked them. Also, when I borrowed Ginger's jacket one evening, I found Dr. Gomez' name and phone number on a piece of paper in the jacket pocket, so I presumed she liked them, too. I wanted to invite a congenial group. Also, I thought it would be nice to become better acquainted with them."

Rhonda thought to herself that she bet that was one party they wished they had not attended.

Aloud she said, "Anita I was so glad you invited Professor Almire. I enjoyed visiting with him again."

"He's a widower, you know, but I don't think he has a chance to get lonesome with all of his kids and grandkids. They're a very close family and they're at his home a lot. He still lives in the same house he has been in for over forty years."

"I suppose the police have been talking to him and to the Gomez family also. Don't you imagine they are questioning all of your dinner guests?"

"Absolutely! Have they been to see you yet?" Anita asked.

"They've honored me with their presence, too!" Rhonda answered, grinning. "I know what you mean about it being embarrassing. I am thankful they come dressed in street clothing and that their siren isn't blaring!"

"Always something to be thankful for!" Anita agreed. "By the way, Ginger told me that you had been married to Ted. I couldn't believe it!"

"I can't believe it, either," Rhonda groaned. "I had hoped she would keep that secret to herself. But no such luck. Apparently Ginger told the police that I was my ex-husband's heir and sole beneficiary, which made me an instant suspect. Probably Suspect NUMBER ONE!"

"We're all suspects, I imagine. I certainly hope they solve this case soon," said Anita."

"I'm surprised that Ginger has stabbed me in the back by telling you and the police about my marriage to Ted. I trusted her. I had been very nice to her, and I had liked her. I was even under the mistaken notion that she had liked me. It seems the people who I have treated the best in my life have been the first to stab me in the back. I've had that happen several times."

"If it's any consolation, people that treat others that way are usually jealous of them. Also, thin-skinned people often take offense from some minor comment when no offense was meant. I try to stay away from that kind of people, and that's good advice for you, too, Rhonda. We don't need people like that in our lives. It's not healthy to be around them. There are too many nice people in the world to waste time on those who make us unhappy, on those we can't trust or depend on."

"You certainly can't depend on most people to do what they say they will do, which is unfortunate," said Rhonda.

"Ginger really made me mad yesterday," Anita confided. "She said she thought I had been interested in Ted."

Rhonda laughed. "I don't mean to be insensitive, but that's ridiculous! Anyone in their right mind would know that you and Felipe only have eyes for each other. When you compare Felipe to Ted, there is no comparison."

"Thank you for saying that. You've made me feel better. But I'll have to admit to you that Felipe was jealous of Ted. He thought Ted flirted with me."

"Anita, don't tell that to anyone else, and especially not to the police." said Rhonda.

Inadvertently Anita had given Felipe a motive for Ted's murder, Rhonda thought to herself. Actually that gave Felipe two motives, since he had been angry at Ted for mistreating his niece, Alejandra. Rhonda pondered these things to herself, but said nothing more on that subject.

"Anita," she asked, "have you seen Ginger since the two of you were college roommates, many moons ago?"

"No, this is the first time I've seen her since our college days, but we have kept in touch. We both like to write letters."

"Did you recognize her? Did she look the same?" Rhonda asked.

"Oh sure, I'd have recognized her anywhere. She looked like she always did, Petite, blonde and blue-eyed."

"What was she like back then?"

"Smart, friendly and cute."

"Good grades?" Rhonda inquired.

"Straight A's!"

"Hobbies?"

"She was a good actress. Often in the school plays, and usually had a main part. She was also artistic, and was excellent at water colors. In fact I had one of her water colors framed. It's in our bedroom. She was very good."

"You and Ginger have certainly had ample time to become reacquainted," said Rhonda. "When does she have to return to work, I wonder? She's having a very long vacation."

"I wonder if she's out of work. No nursing job offers six week vacations."

"She and Ted both appeared to be out of work. Do you think they came here for free room and board?"

"It certainly looks like it, doesn't it?" Anita replied. "I kept wondering why they would stay so long." Changing the subject, she asked, "Would I be impertinent to ask you some questions about Ted?"

"Ask anything you want to know," Rhonda said.

"What kind of a husband was he?"

"Awful! He wouldn't work and support me, and when I complained about it, he would beat me with his fists. Life with him was miserable. I would have left him immediately except I was embarrassed. It was my first year of teaching and I didn't want my student or the other teachers to know about my home life. Back then divorce was not as common as it is today. I wore long sleeves to cover my bruises, and never admitted that my life was not wonderful."

"I'm sorry you had to go through that ordeal. At least you have a good husband, now."

"Yes, Rick is wonderful. I'm very lucky. He's the exact opposite of Ted."

"I couldn't believe Ted was schizophrenic," Anita remarked

"Didn't Ginger tell you that he was mentally ill?"

"No! She didn't! I can't believe she brought a dangerous man into my house. I knew something was wrong."

"Since Ginger told my secret, I don't feel an obligation to her, but I do to you. I told her she should tell you that Ted was paranoid-schizophrenic."

"She certainly did not tell me."

"I'm sorry I didn't tell you, but I was warned to keep my nose out of it. Ted is gone and can't harm either of you, so you might as well not mention it to her."

"Why on earth would you marry a man who was mentally ill, Rhonda?'

"Believe me, I had no idea! If I had known I would never have had one date with him. I would have been too scared! He never told me he had a problem. He was good to me at first. Shall I tell you a little more about Ted?" Rhonda asked.

Anita nodded.

"I was so naive when I married him that I didn't even know how to take birth control pills properly. Apparently I was supposed to have taken them for approximately 20 days, then stop taking them for a certain number of days, but I didn't know I was to stop taking them.

After we had been married a month and my period didn't start, I was frantic because I thought I was pregnant. I was upset for two reasons. One, I was afraid my relatives and acquaintances would think that I had to get married if I was pregnant so soon, and secondly, Ted had apparently had a relapse, had quit his job and had beaten me when I complained. By now, I knew the marriage was a terrible mistake and I certainly did not want to have his baby.

So I went to the doctor who had prescribed the pills and told him I thought I was pregnant.

He asked, "When did you stop taking the pills?"

I replied that I hadn't stopped taking them, that I was still taking them.

He burst into laughter and told me I couldn't be pregnant if I was still taking them and hadn't missed a pill. He said I had to stop taking them before my period could start.

Wow! did I breathe a sigh of relief! I was so thankful!"

Anita laughed at the anecdote, then asked, "Did you tell Ted before you went to the doctor that you might be pregnant? How did he react?"

"Do you know what he said to me when I told him? He grabbed my hair, yanked it and yelled that I'd have to get rid of it, that he had no intention of working two jobs to support a brat! At the time, he wasn't even working one job. Then he began hitting me and kicking me in the stomach."

Anita hugged Rhonda. "I'm so sorry you had to endure that. Before I talked to you today I had felt sorry about Ted's death. Now I see he was no loss to this earth. Only scum would have reacted in such a way. I wouldn't have blamed you if you had killed him!"

They sat there in silence for a few minutes, then finally Rhonda changed the subject and asked, "Have you talked to Juanita lately?"

"Yesterday. She said she also is being harassed by the police. Of course, we realize they are just doing their job."

"Is Juanita doing OK? I only see her at church. I've been meaning to have her over for dinner. She's such a nice woman."

"Yes, she is, and I know she would enjoy having dinner with you. She's a widow, you know, and probably lonely. I invited Professor Almire to dinner that fateful evening in the hope that they might get better acquainted."

Rhonda laughed, "So you're a match maker in your spare time!"

Anita grinned, "Yes, and you ought to invite him to your house the night you ask Juanita. Maybe if we work on it together, we'll be successful."

"He's a wonderful man, but isn't he about fifteen years older than she?"

"What difference does that make? He's young in spirit!"

"Ok. I'll ask them both if it will make you happy," Rhonda answered, amused.

"It will," she smiled. Then her expression changed and she said, "Rhonda, what are we going to do if the police don't solve the murder soon? Do you know they have even questioned our maid? Actually she isn't really a maid. She's Felipe's niece and she's helping us out to make extra money while she is in college."

"I guess they have to question everyone who was in your house that evening."

"I'm very upset and somewhat embarrassed to tell you this, but the police came to our house with a search warrant yesterday afternoon and searched it from top to bottom. They left no stone untouched."

"What a waste of time!" Rhonda exclaimed. "Of course they wouldn't find anything in your home."

"Frankly, I think it was because of Ginger that they conducted such a thorough search."

"Of course it was," Rhonda agreed. She did not mention that her own home had been searched and what they had found.

"There's something I'm curious about, Rhonda. Why did Carlos ask you to bring the dessert and even suggest which one you should take?"

"He suggested I take his favorite dessert if I was planning to take one."

"You don't think he would have planned to sprinkle only enough arsenic over the dessert to make Ted sick, not meaning to kill him, do you?"

"Oh Anita, Carlos, didn't even know Ted. He'd only seen him twice in his life."

"I've heard that Carlos has a bad temper and likes to get even with people who have crossed him," she replied.

"How would Ted have crossed Carlos? He'd never met him until that night at our party."

"I thought you might know if he had a grudge against Ted," Anita replied primly.

When Rhonda didn't reply, Anita continued, "He did give Ted some pills and Ted died after taking them."

"Ted died from arsenic poisoning, as you well know. Carlos gave Ted two Pepcid pills for his upset stomach as a friendly, helpful gesture," Rhonda replied, exasperated. "And you may rest assured that the pills had not been soaked in poison."

"How do we know that Ted didn't die from two arsenic pills, and not from an arsenic powder sprinkled over his dessert?"

"I never heard of arsenic in pill form. Did you?"

"No but I don't know anything about arsenic."

"Neither does Carlos! Apparently it doesn't pay to try to be kind." Rhonda replied, angrily.

'I apologize for mentioning this suspicion to you, Rhonda. I didn't mean to make you angry."

"I'd certainly like to know who put such nonsense into your head."

Anita replied, "It was Juanita."

# Chapter Twenty-One

The next morning a box of chocolates arrived in the mail for Rhonda. "I wonder who these can be from?" she asked Rick and Carlos.

"Isn't there a card enclosed with the package?" Rick asked.

"No. Isn't that curious?" Maybe I have a secret admirer?" she laughed.

"Rhonda, I don't think you'd better eat any of them," said Rick. "What do you think, Carlos?"

"I think you should give the box to Javier or to Agente Sola and ask them to send it to the lab to be analyzed."

"Good idea. Let's don't take any chances, said Rick. "Someone has already tried to 'set you up' by leaving that packet in your desk."

"A person who has once killed will often kill again. We must all be very careful until this case is solved," said Carlos. "I read an article in the paper recently about two bottles of cyanide-laced wine being sent to a couple through the mail. The both drank it and died."

"You've convinced me Carlos! I'm not touching these chocolates," she shuddered. "Let's change the subject. Is it OK with you two if I invite Juanita and professor Almire here for dinner Saturday night?"

"They might not want to come here. Remember you are the one who made the Chocolate Death dessert," Rick said.

"You're right. Maybe I'd better put that idea on the back burner and wait until the case is solved to invite them."

Later that afternoon Javier phoned and kiddingly told Rhonda that he had heard she was the 'Miss Marple' of Guanajuato.

"I'll bet I can guess who you have been talking to," she laughed. "It couldn't have been Agente Rivera from San Miguel, could it?"

He chuckled, "How did you guess? But seriously he told me you are the 'Cat's Meow,' and that I'd better take your name off my suspect list!"

"That is good news! I feel like my head is slowly sliding out of the noose."

"He also told me to pick your brain and go along with any suggestions you might come up with. He said you had a real screwy idea concerning a case he was working on last summer, and he only let you try it because he was desperate. He said that your idea solved the case, and he got the credit for it, which made his points go up at the Ministerio Publico in San Miguel!"

"After such a wonderful testimonial, I wish I had an idea for you, screwy or otherwise," said Rhonda. "But unfortunately my mind is as blank as a sheet of typing paper. However, I do have something to tell you. We had a little excitement here this morning when the postman came. He brought a mysterious box of chocolates to me. Since there was no card enclosed and no return address for the sender, Rick and Carlos won't let me have even one bite. Carlos was telling me a story of some cyanide-laced wine delivered through the mail which made me lose my taste for chocolate, temporarily at least."

"I'm going to send Alcocer or Sola over to pick up the chocolates. We'll run it through our lab. If it tests OK, you can have it back and gorge on chocolate to your heart's content!"

"Thanks. I'll feel safer if you do that," she replied.

"Be glad to," he said. "By the way, I heard some interesting gossip about you, Rhonda!"

"I'll bet I can guess what it was! You heard I was Ted's first wife and the sole beneficiary of his will."

"You got it, Bubbles!"

Rhonda burst out laughing. "I'm never going to live that nickname down! Hope it doesn't get printed in the newspaper, but it probably will if Ginger has anything to do with it!"

"We've talked to Ginger about the sugar packet hidden in your desk, and she admitted that she put it there, but at Ted's request. She insisted that Ted had given it to her the day she came to your home for lunch and that he had told her to hide it in a place where you wouldn't find it until they had returned to the States. She said she thought the envelope had contained a note or letter to you from Ted, and even though the fact that he wrote to you made her angry and jealous, she insisted that she wouldn't think of reading someone else's mail."

"So that was what she was doing in my office when she was supposed to have been consulting over the phone with Dr. Gomez about Ted's mental problems!" exclaimed Rhonda.

"You suspected it was she who planted the evidence, didn't you?" he asked.

"Of course! She was the only person who has spent time alone in my office. Who else could it have been?"

"Ginger swore that she did not know the envelope contained arsenic and that she would never have planted something like that in your home."

"Sure!" Rhonda said sarcastically.

"Do you think Ginger killed Ted?" he asked. "She was sitting closest to him."

Rhonda replied, "If Ginger had been married to Ted for five or ten years and had been through several remissions and relapses of his mental illness with him, and if he had been involved in love affairs behind her back--or if she had been in love with another man, then maybe she would have done it. She would have had a motive. But as it is, they are newly married, she has shown no interest in other men that I'm aware of, and she appeared to be in love with Ted. What is her motive?"

"I've heard gossip that she was interested in another man," he said, "though I shouldn't tell you."

"I suppose you heard she had a crush on Felipe. That's nonsense. She would be wasting her time. Anita and Felipe appear to be very happy."

"'Appear' is the definitive word," he said. "Things are not always the way they 'appear' to be."

"That is the problem with this case. All of the suspects 'appear' to be so nice. I can't imagine any of them as cold blooded killers."

"Neither can I," agreed Javier. "But someone is not nice. Call me if you get an idea or discover a clue. So long, Bubbles!"

A few minutes after Javier hung up, Camila returned from her assignment at the Gomez home. With Carlos translating, she said, "Elisa mentioned that she had overheard Marta and Francisco discussing the poisoning of some man at a dinner party they had attended. They had talked about each of the guests, wondering which one did it and why. They seemed to think the murder had something to do with a serious mental illness.

Elisa also admitted that she had heard them arguing another time about some woman.

Marta accused him of having a love affair. He denied it, and Marta called him a liar. Elisa had no idea who the woman was or why Marta thought he was fooling around, but she said she had heard that sometimes, psychiatrists have affairs with their patients, so that might have been what happened."

"Did Elisa say what caused Marta to believe the gossip about her husband?" Rhonda asked. "Did she say who the woman was?"

"No. I asked her that question," Camila replied, "but she

said she didn't hear all of the argument. She did say that she was very surprised, because she had always thought that they were happily married, and that this was the first time she had ever heard anything about an extramarital affair."

Camila summed up her conversation with Elisa by stating that getting information out of Elisa was like pulling teeth. "You won't believe how hard I had to work to get that little bit of information. Elisa is very fond of them, and she didn't want to say anything which could hurt them."

"Did you ask if they had any arsenic in the greenhouse?" Carlos wanted to know.

"Yes. I told her we needed to borrow some to kill the weeds by the bougainvillas. She didn't know if there was any or not so I volunteered to go with her and look for some."

"And did you find it?" asked Carlos.

"Yes, we did."

After thanking Camila for the good work and promising her a bonus in her weekly paycheck, Rhonda went to the kitchen and began to prepare dinner.

Carlos followed her. "What are you cooking, Bubbles?"

She giggled, "Get out of here if you're going to call me that name!"

Ignoring him, she rinsed four boneless, skinless chicken breast halves and patted them dry with paper towels. After spraying a pan with a cooking spray, she arranged the chicken in one layer, then poured a cup of orange juice over it.

"Ah, you're baking Orange Onion Chicken, I see. Here's the onion soup mix." He opened it and sprinkled half of the package over the chicken, then took the pan from her and placed it in a 350 degree F oven.

"What are you serving with it?" he asked.

"Dressing, Cranberry salad, green beans and cherry-chocolate cake."

## Orange-Onion Chicken

4-6 chicken breast halves,
skinned and boned

1/2 to 1 package dry
onion soup mix
1 cup orange juice

Trim all visible fat from chicken. Spray a 9x13 inch pan with a non-stick cooking spray, then arrange chicken pieces in the pan. Pour orange juice over chicken, then sprinkle with dry onion soup mix.

Bake 30 minutes at 350 degrees F. Turn chicken. (Optional: Spoon orange marmalade over chicken.) Bake 20 to 30 minutes longer, or until tender. Serves 4-6.

Note: It is not necessary to turn chicken.

## Easy Dressing

1 (6 oz) box Stove Top corn
bread stuffing mix

1 (10 1/2 oz) can chicken
broth
1 chopped onion

Combine stuffing mix, the contents of the vegetable seasoning packet (that comes with the stuffing), the chopped onion, and the broth in a mixing bowl and mix well.

Spray a baking dish with a non-stick cooking spray. Pour dressing into prepared dish and bake at 325 degrees F for 30 minutes.

Optional: Add chopped celery to dressing before baking.

## Creamy Cranberry Salad

2 (3 oz) pkg. cherry Jell-O
1 cup sour cream

1 (16 oz) can jellied
cranberry sauce

Dissolve Jell-O in 2 cups boiling water. Stir in cranberry sauce. Mix until well blended. Add sour cream and beat in an electric mixer until creamy. Pour into a mold and chill until firm. Serves 6 to 8.

## Audrey's Green Beans

1 (15 oz) can cut green beans
1 Tablespoon Lipton's dry
onion soup mix

1 tsp olive oil

Combine the 3 ingredients in a saucepan. Heat slowly until liquid is cooked up, stirring occasionally. Note: For faster green beans partially drain then add olive oil and onion mix. Bring to a boil. Reduce heat and cook 5 minutes, stirring occasionally. Serves 4.

## Chocolate Cherry Cake

1 box Duncan Hines devils
food cake mix
2 large eggs

1 (21 oz) can cherry pie
filling

Combine and mix cake mix and eggs. Stir in cherry pie filling. Mix until well blended. Pour into a greased and floured 9x13 inch pan and bake for 35 to 40 minutes at 350 degrees F. For 2 (9 inch) cake pans, bake for 25 to 35 minutes. For Bundt pan, bake for 40-50 minutes.Frost as desired. Serves 8.

Optional: Serve with a dip of ice cream. Drizzle chocolate syrup over all.

Teatro Juárez and the Church of San Diego

# Chapter Twenty-Two

Ginger phoned the next morning and asked, "Rhonda, can I come to your house? I have something to tell you."

Irritated at her for telling her secret to anyone who would listen and for planting the arsenic in her desk, Rhonda's reply was cool. "Can't you tell me over the phone? I'm busy now."

"I guess I can," Ginger sighed. "Nobody is here except the maid, and she is in the kitchen." She paused, then said in a low voice, "I think I know who killed Ted."

Rhonda bit her tongue. She was tempted to ask if she was Ginger's suspect, since Ginger had certainly tried to implicate her. Instead she merely asked, "Who?"

"Just two days before Ted's death, he told me he didn't feel as close to God as he once had and that he needed to talk to a minister about his salvation. Since he felt Felipe didn't like him, he was hesitant to talk to him. Instead he decided to go to Juanita's house. Anita had once taken us to Juanita's home for lunch, so he knew where she lived. Since she was a Sunday School teacher and since she had been friendly to him, he felt free to talk to her.

He should have phoned her to ask if she was free to talk to him, but you know Ted. He was always impulsive. So he walked to her house and knocked several times on her door. Then when she didn't answer, he tried the door knob and it opened. He thought he would go inside, find pen and paper and leave a note for her asking her to phone him."

"Was he planning to leave the note inside her house?" Rhonda asked. "If so, she would know he had been inside, uninvited."

"No. He said he planned to write the note, then go outside,

close the door, and slip the note under her door. However, things didn't turn out that way. When he walked in he didn't see either paper or a pencil, so he decided to look for them in her bedroom.

When he opened her bedroom door, there were three very surprised people: Ted, Juanita and Dr. Gomez! You get my meaning, don't you?" she asked. Then as if she thought Rhonda was too dumb to understand, Ginger explained. "Juanita and Dr. Gomez were in bed! Ted said they looked like Adam and Eve without the fig leaves!"

"Ginger, that's hard for me to believe! Poor Marta!" She exclaimed.

Ginger continued, "I watched them the night of the dinner party. They sat across the table from each other. I couldn't see the doctor very well from where I sat, but I could see Juanita quite well, and she couldn't keep her eyes off of him."

"Ginger, are you sure Ted really saw them together? Sometimes he tells stories that aren't true. We both know that."

"I believe Ted was telling the truth about what he saw," Ginger said, "and I think that's why he was killed. They were afraid he would tell Marta and Felipe, and they certainly didn't want that story to get around! It would damage their reputations and Marta would probably have divorced Francisco. Also, I'm sure Felipe would never have let Juanita continue to teach Sunday School if he heard about it."

"Do you think Ted would have tried to blackmail both of them?" Rhonda asked.

"Who knows? He's been out of a job for quite a while, and consequently, short on money. He probably thought Dr. Gomez was wealthy since two doctors in one family should be doing quite well financially. He did not tell me that he threatened to blackmail them, but he might have seen this as an opportunity for some fast, easy money."

"Do you think one of them might have poisoned Ted that night of the dinner party?" Rhonda inquired.

"I certainly do!"

"How could either one of them have done it? Both sat at the other end of the table, nowhere near Ted."

"Remember the diversion caused by Marta's lost earring? I think that Francisco 'accidentally on purpose' knocked it off of her ear. It was a clip-on earring so it could easily have fallen off after a slight nudge. Then when everyone was scrambling around on the floor looking for it, Francisco could have gotten up, pretending to see if it fell behind his or one of the neighboring chairs and then when nobody was paying attention, he took advantage of the opportunity and sprinkled arsenic on my poor Ted's dessert."

"Of course, that's possible, Ginger, but I don't want to believe it. I like them both so much."

"I like them, too," she said, "but if either one murdered my husband, they're certainly going to pay."

"Actually it's their word against Ted's" said Rhonda, "and when push comes to shove who do you think a Mexican jury is going to believe--a Mexican doctor and teacher or an American schizophrenic patient? Besides, I don't believe Francisco and Juanita would commit murder and risk life imprisonment."

"I disagree with you," Ginger stated, "and you may rest assured that my testimony in court will be very convincing."

"But your testimony is based on hearsay. You didn't actually see Francisco poison Ted's food."

Ginger asked, "Didn't I?"

Museum of the Mummies
Museo de las Momias

# Chapter Twenty-Three

Rhonda was walking her poodle, Cleopatra, along Guanajuato Boulevard when a car pulled alongside her and stopped. Frightened she increased her pace, but stopped when she heard a man call her name. She was relieved to see Dr. Gomez at the wheel, waving at her.

She walked to his car and leaned down to see him better. "How are you?" she smiled.

"Fine. Seeing you saves me from phoning you. Marta and I are going to a concert at the Teatro Juarez on Saturday night, and we would like to invite Rick, Carlos and you to be our guests if you are available."

"Thank you, I'd love to go, and I'm sure Carlos and Rick would enjoy it, too. I'll talk to them and phone you tonight to tell you for sure."

"I'll talk to you later then. Bye Rhonda."

That evening Rhonda told the guys about her talks with both Javier and Ginger.

"This is in strictest confidence. I hope none of this will be repeated to anyone."

"Of course not," they both agreed.

"I was certain Ginger had hidden the packet," said Rick.

"So was I," Carlos nodded. "Who else could it have been? Don't you think her alibi was a bit weak? Ted isn't around to deny that he told her to do it."

"Why would Ted want arsenic placed in the desk?"

"It doesn't make sense to me," Rick said, then added, "unless he planned to kill himself and he wanted to frame you, wanted the police to think you had done him in."

"Why would he want to pin it on me? I haven't done

anything to him. That may be why he made me heir to his 'five peso fortune'! He knew his heir would be a suspect.

I can't understand why he would frame me. In retrospect, I was good to him. I paid for his room and board for the year we were married. Unwillingly, of course."

"You know how people are. They don't remember what you have done for them in the past. They only remember what you are not doing for them at the moment," Rick remarked.

"Knowing you, I can't believe you were the timid wife you portray when talking about Ted beating you," said Carlos, a grin on his face. "Tell us what you really did to him when he hit you."

"Usually I had my arms wrapped around my head trying to protect what brains I had."

Carlos looked skeptical, "What did you do to him when you weren't protecting 'those little gray cells'?"

"Once when he hit me, I grabbed a clothes hanger and hit him in the mouth with it. The last time I saw him, I noticed he still had a chipped tooth!" she reported proudly.

"Now, she's starting to sound like the Rhonda I know!" Rick grinned. "What else did you do to him?"

"Once when he hit me I was in the kitchen, so I grabbed a skillet and hit him over the head with it."

"Did you ever chase him with a baseball bat?" Rick asked, amused.

"Just twice. Then he threw it in a creek!"

Carlos said with a droll Jack Benny expression on his face, "I can't understand why Ted would try to frame her, can you, Rick?"

"No way! She was always so good to him!"

"If you smart alecks aren't nice to me I won't tell you the gossip Ginger told me," Rhonda said, changing the subject.

"Who was it about?" Rick inquired.

"She said Ted caught Dr. Gomez in Juanita's bed!"

"By himself?"

"Nope! Juanita was with him!"

"And he blackmailed Dr. Gomez, so the good doctor had to kill him. Is that what we're supposed to believe?" Rick asked, a skeptical expression on his face.

"Maybe it's true," said Carlos. "People will surprise you!"

"Which reminds me," said Rhonda, "I saw Dr. Gomez a few minutes ago and he invited the three of us to a concert Saturday night. Shall we go?"

"Why not? He won't poison us at a concert," said Carlos.

"Are you sure? Couldn't he give us an injection of strychnine?" Rhonda joked.

Saturday soon rolled around and everyone seemed to enjoy the concert. Afterwards Dr. Gomez suggested they walk across the street to Valadez Restaurant for a snack.

After a short, discussion of the music and the musicians, the conversation turned to Ted's murder.

"Apparently, I'm the number one suspect," Rhonda groaned. "I'll certainly be thankful when this case is solved. Maybe I can salvage what's left of my reputation."

"If we thought you were the culprit, Rhonda, we would never have invited you out for the evening," Marta consoled her.

"You've made me feel much better," Rhonda smiled. "Thank you."

"I wonder what makes some people turn violent," Rick mused.

Dr. Gomez replied, "I believe, that though childhood abuse can be a factor, that some people are born with the tendency to be violent."

"They're just born mean?" Rhonda asked.

"Studies have found there is a link between violence and

brain dysfunction," he said, "so, in a way, I guess you could say they were born mean."

"Are you saying a person can't help being violent if they have a brain dysfunction?"

"This is only my opinion, but I believe they have some degree of control, that they have freedom of choice. However the deficit may leave individuals with an emotionally blunted personality lacking in conscience development."

Rick asked, "Do you think the person who killed Ted may have done so due to a brain dysfunction and may not be 100% responsible for his action?"

"I think that's a possibility," the doctor replied.

"If Ted was killed, that is," Marta said. "Personally, I think it was suicide."

They were silent a few minutes, each thinking their own thoughts about Marta's comment, then Rhonda said, "Let's talk about something pleasant. Rick and I are excited because we are going to see our son in eight days. We haven't seen him since January."

"Wonderful," Marta smiled. "Is he in college or has he graduated?"

"He's just a freshman at Baylor University in Waco."

"I hope you'll introduce him to us while he's here," said Dr. Gomez.

"We certainly will," Rick replied.

"Let me show you his picture," Rhonda said, "pulling his photo out of her billfold.

"Very handsome," the two doctors agreed after seeing his picture.

"Thanks. And here's a picture of our daughter, Nikki."

"She's beautiful!" Marta exclaimed.

"She certainly is," Francisco agreed, then asked, "When will she be here for a visit?"

"Soon, I hope. She's married and lives in San Antonio with her husband."

"Do you have any grandchildren?" Marta asked.

"None yet. Nikki said they wanted to wait five years, and they've only been married one and a half years. Do you two have children and grandchildren?"

"We have a daughter, Gabriella, and a grandson, Luis, who live near here, so we get to see them at least once monthly or more."

"That's great. I wish we got to see our kids that often. You're lucky!"

"Are your children good about writing letters?" Marta asked.

"No. I give them a bunch of stamped, addressed post cards every time we see them. All they have to do is jot a few lines on the back and mail them. If I didn't do that, I'd probably never get a letter, unfortunately," Rhonda complained. "They certainly didn't take after me. I like to write letters and I write them often."

Rick grinned, "She's insinuating they inherited my writing genes!"

That evening after they returned home, when Rhonda was preparing to do the laundry, she checked all pockets so kleenex, etcetera would not go through the wash. She was shocked to find a sugar packet in the pocket of one of Carlos' pair of slacks. She removed it and hid it until she could decide what should be done with it. She wondered if he was being framed or if he was not the person she had thought he was. She naturally became suspicious of him and was determined to watch his every move.

She told Rick about it that night, but he refused to believe that Carlos had put the packet in his pocket.

"He was framed the same way you were," he said.

"I'm sure you are right, Rick. I'll bet he was as suspicious of me when the police found the arsenic in my desk as I was of him when I found the sugar in his pocket, but he was nice enough not to ever mention it."

# Chapter Twenty-Four

On Sunday morning, April 5, the Reverend Felipe Lopez spoke on the subject of lying.

The week before he had told his congregation, "Next week I will preach about the sin of lying. To help you understand my sermon, I want all of you this week to read Mark Chapter 17."

Today, as he prepared to deliver his sermon he asked for a show of hands to see how many had read Mark 17.

Many hands went up.

Felipe, amused, then smiled and said, "The Book of Mark has only 16 Chapters. I will now continue my sermon on the sin of lying."

After the sermon was over and they were leaving the church, they shook hands with Felipe and Rick said, "Good sermon. That trick certainly got everyone's attention."

Felipe laughed, "Did you raise your hand, Rick?"

"I can vouch for him," Rhonda giggled. "He did not raise his hand! I don't think he ever told a lie in his whole life!"

On the way home Jimmy asked, "Did anyone notice if Ginger raised her hand?"

That afternoon, after lunch, Rick and Rhonda began receiving harassing hang-up phone calls.

After the seventh or eighth call Rick said, "How I wish for caller-ID!"

"We don't have it in Guanajuato yet," Carlos replied.

"Doesn't matter," said Rhonda. "The caller would surely know how to block the name and phone number from the screen. It would probably read "Unavailable" or "anonymous" or "no data sent!"

"Shall we unplug the phone and end the caller's fun for this afternoon?" Carlos asked.

On Monday after Rhonda returned home from the University, the phone was plugged in again and the hang-up phone calls started once more.

"Carlos, would you call the phone company and see if they can put a tracer on this line?"

"I will," he replied, "but they might not do anything without an order from the police department."

"Then let's just let it go for now. I'll phone Javier later and ask him what can be done," Rhonda said.

"Who do you think is calling?" Rick asked. "I've heard it's usually someone you know when they don't talk."

"It has to be someone from the dinner party. I imagine it's Ginger. She's upset that I'm Ted's heir and this is her way of working off her anger. Boy is she a pain! People sure can fool you! I used to think she was nice."

"Maybe it's not Ginger," Carlos said. "It could be an angry student who got a bad grade. I had a problem like that with a student a few years ago."

"None of my students flunked. They all seriously want to learn to speak English and they've worked hard. The lowest grade I gave was a 'C'."

They left the phone plugged in and went to a movie, leaving their mysterious caller to let the phone ring to his or her heart's content.

Javier phoned the next morning. "I have news about your chocolates, Bubbles!" he greeted her.

Rhonda giggled, "Javier, you're a nut! Were they poisoned or not?"

"No, they weren't. That doesn't make sense, does it?"

It's probably a form of harassment. We'll eventually learn why it was sent, I suppose."

"Living in Guanajuato has been a barrel of fun! Now, I'm getting hang-up phone calls. Dozens of them. We have to keep the phone unplugged at night or we wouldn't get a wink of sleep."

"Someone does love you, Bubbles! You sure know how to make friends!"

"Any chance the police department can have a tracer put on my line?"

"Sure. I'll see to it now. Do you want this candy?"

"No thanks! Just pitch them! I've lost my taste for chocolate."

"OK. Have a good day!" he said.

"I am going to because my son is coming for Easter vacation on Friday."

"I'm happy for you, Bubbles! You could use some good news," he said, then hung up the receiver before she could complain again about his nickname for her.

On Friday Jimmy flew to Mexico City, then changed planes and flew on to Silao, near Guanajuato. Rhonda, Rick and Carlos were at the airport to meet him. Jimmy hugged them all and said, "I'm sure happy to see you guys!"

During the drive home they told him about all of the excitement. "Never a dull moment," Rick said.

They entertained Jimmy with stories about his mother, better known as "Bubbles," who had in a few short months, managed to become a prime suspect in a murder case, her murdered ex-husband's heir, the recipient of a mysterious box of chocolates and numerous harassing phone calls.

"Mom, you're living an interesting life!" Jimmy teased. "I talked to Nikki last week and she said the police had searched the house and found arsenic in your desk. If you keep this up they'll call you the 'Lizzie Borden' of Guanajuato!"

"Lizzie used an ax, not arsenic!" Rhonda informed him,"

So they'd better not call me that. In comparison to that name, Bubbles is starting to sound good."

When they arrived home, they were surprised to see shattered glass laying on the sidewalk in front of their house.

"Ginger has struck again!" Rhonda exclaimed. "This time she's broken a window!"

They went on inside and sure enough they found a rock on the balcony outside of the broken window.

"This is not funny," Rhonda complained, then she went to the phone and dialed Javier's phone number to report this newest incident.

He told her that the telephone company had put a tracer on her line and that the phone calls were coming from various pay phones. "Apparently someone doesn't have enough to do to keep themselves occupied," he said.

"I think that 'someone' is Ginger. Who else has time to traipse around town from one pay phone to another? I wish you could put a tail on her."

"So do I, but it's too expensive, and so far these incidents are merely annoying, not life threatening."

After Rhonda was off the phone, Carlos said, "I have an idea. Remember the man who was the night watchman while your house was under construction?"

Rhonda nodded.

"Why don't you hire him to "tail" or follow Ginger at a discreet distance without her being aware of it? He will be able to tell us if she makes phone calls from a pay phone, and you can be at home to take any call which might come in. In that way we can catch her, or at least determine whether or not she is our culprit. If so, we can turn our evidence in to the police."

Jimmy said, "Since she doesn't know me, I could shadow her."

"No way!" Rhonda said. "This woman could be dangerous. I absolutely will not allow you to do it. But the idea is a good one, Carlos." She then turned to Rick and asked, "What do you think? Shall we hire that night watchman?"

"Absolutely. We have to do something. Can you contact him today, Carlos?"

"Sure, but first I'd better call someone to replace the window."

The man was hired to tail Ginger, and he began the next day. Where Ginger went, he went. He reported that she had not been to a pay phone all day Saturday, and Rhonda who had sat by the phone all day, reported that she had not received a single harassing, hang-up phone call all day.

"Is that coincidence or not?" Rhonda asked. "Personally, I think she knows he is following her."

"Looks suspicious," Rick agreed.

"It's worth the money to keep Ginger away from the pay phones," Rhonda said. "Let's keep him on the payroll."

The watchman was told to report "for work" at 12:30 on Easter Sunday, after the service was over at church. He reported at the end of the day that Ginger had gone to a restaurant for lunch with Anita and Felipe, and to church with them that evening. She had not been alone all day, and coincidentally, Rhonda and Rick received no hang-up phone calls.

"Don't you think that is evidence that Ginger is making the calls?" Rhonda asked. "She apparently knows she is being followed and that's why the phone calls have stopped."

"I'm having an exciting vacation," Jimmy said sarcastically. "Sitting by the phone waiting for it to ring is nearly as much fun as watching paint dry."

"Let's take him to a movie tonight," Carlos suggested. "We've got to entertain this boy!"

"And feed him, too," said Rhonda. "Tell me Jimmy, what

do you want me to cook for you tomorrow?"

"That's easy, Mom. I'm hungry for your lemon roast, potatoes, corn, carrots, cherry Jello and chocolate pie."

"Then will you walk to town with me to buy the groceries?"

"Sure, Mom. Shall we walk to Pipila and take the steps down the mountain side?"

"Of course. That's the fast way."

If Jimmy hadn't been with her, Rhonda might have reached the bottom of the hill much faster than she had planned.

### Lemon Rump Roast

1 (2 to 3 lb) rump roast or          1 cup lemon juice
    eye of round (boneless)          1/2 tsp lemon pepper

Trim all visible fat from meat. Place rump roast in a Pyrex dish. Prick top of roast with a fork. Pour lemon juice over roast. Rub juice into the meat. Cover and refrigerate 6 hours or overnight. Turn 2 to 3 times. Drain off juice; sprinkle meat with lemon pepper. Place in a baking dish, cover and roast at 325 degree F until desired degree of doneness is reached.

### Potato Casserole

5 potatoes, peeled and sliced          1 (10 3/4 oz) can cream
1 cup grated Cheddar cheese              of mushroom soup

Place a layer of sliced potatoes in a greased casserole dish. Pour soup, that has been diluted with water, over the potatoes. Mix well. Bake for 45 minutes at 400 degrees F, covered. Uncover; top with cheese and bake for 15 minutes longer. Optional: Add onions before baking.

### Creamed Corn

1 large box frozen whole
    kernel corn
Lemon pepper to taste

8 oz cream cheese,
    softened

Cook corn according to package directions; drain. Stir cream cheese into hot corn; stir until melted and well heated. Season to taste with lemon pepper.

### Ritzy Carrot Casserole

2 (16 oz) cans carrots
    drained and heated
1 tube crushed Ritz crackers

1 small jar Cheez Whiz,
    melted

Drain heated carrots and pour them into a greased baking dish. Top with melted Cheez Whiz. Spread crushed Ritz crackers over carrots. Bake at 300 degrees F, until golden brown.

### Cherry Berry Salad

1 (6 oz) pkg cherry Jell-O
1 (15 oz) can whole berry
    cranberry sauce

1 (10 oz) pkg frozen
    strawberries

Dissolve Jell-O as package directs in 2 cups boiling water, mixing well. Stir in undrained strawberries and whole berry cranberry sauce. Pour into 7x11 inch glass dish and refrigerate until set. Serves 8 to 10. Optional: Frost firm gelatin with sour cream.

## Chocolate Almond Pie

1 (8 oz) Hershey's chocolate almond bar

1 (8 inch) graham cracker prepared crust
1 small tub Cool Whip

Melt Hershey's bar in top of double boiler over hot water. Remove from heat and cool. Stir Cool Whip into chocolate. Fill the pie crust and chill. Top with additional Cool Whip, if desired.

Optional: Garnish by using a potato peeler to shave chocolate curls off a Hershey's candy bar. Serves 6 to 8.

# Chapter Twenty-Five

As Rhonda and Jimmy walked toward the statue of Pipila he said, "Mom, let's climb to the top of Pipila. I've never done it."

She agreed, and they climbed the steps to the top where they could see a spectacular panoramic view of downtown Guanajuato and the surrounding mountains.

"What a magnificent view!" she exclaimed. Her eyes were only on the view. She vaguely noticed there were other people milling around, but she paid no attention to them.

"Are you ready to climb down, Mom?" Jimmy asked.

She nodded and they began the descent. Other people fell in line behind them, then one person accidentally tripped and fell foreward against Rhonda, causing her to lose her balance and start to fall. If it hadn't been for Jimmy's quick reflex of grabbing her, she could have fallen and rolled to the bottom of the steps, severely injuring or killing herself. He steadied her and they slowly walked down the remaining stairs and outside.

Though Rhonda was still shaking, she hugged Jimmy. "Thank you, darling. You probably saved my life or kept me from breaking both legs!"

He seemed thoughtful. "Mom, I'm not sure that was an accident. I think you were pushed. After I grabbed you, one of the people behind us shoved me to the side and raced past us and on down the stairs. I couldn't identify the person. I just have an impression of a woman wearing jeans and a baseball cap."

"Did she have blonde hair?" Rhonda asked.

"I didn't see any hair. It was all tucked under her cap. It

all happened so fast, so I don't remember anymore about it."

"Jimmy, I'm scared. Now that I think back on the incident, I'm sure I was pushed. I can almost feel her hands shove me."

"We are going back home, Mom. I'm not going to let you walk down the steps embedded in that mountain side. Somebody could be hiding behind a bush or a tree, waiting for you. If you got pushed down some areas of that descent, you might not stop rolling until you get to the jardin de la union!"

"You've convinced me. We'll go home and send Rick to the grocery store."

As they walked home Jimmy asked, "Do you think it was Ginger who pushed you?"

"Who else could it be?" she asked.

"Last night Dad said there were five women at the party, but that you suspect Ginger of everything because she put the envelope in your desk. He said it could easily be one of the other women, that they may have a motive you aren't aware of."

They arrived home, and explained what had happened at the Pipila Monument.

"How long has it been since you've talked to Nikki?" Jimmy asked his mother.

"Two weeks. We spoke on March 30, and they were to call us when they learn something about Ted and Ginger," replied his father.

"I phoned them on Easter, but they weren't home, so I left them a message, wishing them a Happy Easter, on their answering machine." said Rhonda.

Carlos asked, "Didn't they say the man with the information would be off work for about one or two weeks?"

Rick nodded. "I hope he's getting along OK."

"Let's call her," suggested Jimmy, "I miss her a lot."

"You can call," said Rhonda. If I were depending on them

to save me from the noose, I'd be in trouble."

The next morning, about 8:00 the doorbell rang and it was Camila.

Carlos said, "Hi Mata Hari. Are you ready to go sleuthing again?"

"Sure. Where do you want me to go?"

Carlos turned to Rhonda and Rick. "Do you want her to try again?"

"Sure," said Rick. "That leaves the professor and Juanita."

He asked Camila if she knew their maids.

"I know one maid in the professor's home, but nobody at Señora Juanita's home."

"Then go to the professor's home and find out everything you can."

"You know he's not guilty," said Rhonda."

"He's the least suspicious person and he seems to have lived an exemplary life, but the least suspicious person is often the one "whodunit" in the mystery novels."

"It can't hurt anything," said Rick. "She might as well go. I'll drop her off." He turned to Rhonda, "If you're ready to go. I'll drive you to the University."

"Thanks. Shall I take a taxi home or will you be able to pick me up?"

"I'll pick you up. I really don't think you ought to be out of my sight. The person who is after you is getting braver each day."

"You scare me when you talk like that," Rhonda complained as they got into the car.

"I think you need to be scared so you'll be more careful. I'm getting worried. Have you told Javier about this last attempt?"

"No, but I plan to talk to him this afternoon."

"I'm going to sit in the back of your class and read a novel," Rick declared. "I'm not going to let you go anywhere without me until this case is solved."

Later that afternoon after lunch Rhonda was at her home sitting in her office trying to write on her novel, but she was having trouble concentrating. "I might as well give up," she thought to herself a minute before the telephone rang.

"Ah, a welcome diversion," she said aloud, then answered. It was Nikki.

"Hi Sweetheart, I'm happy to hear from you," she said.

"Mom, Jimmy called yesterday and fussed at me because we hadn't gotten the information you requested, so I made Juan do it today. He's been awfully busy."

"And I've been harassed daily and could have been killed yesterday," she replied.

"I'll let you talk to Juan now," she said.

Juan said he had quite a lot of information, so she grabbed a notebook and took notes as he talked, sometimes asking him to repeat sentences and sometimes questioning him to be certain she understood correctly the points he was making. She then read her notes back to him to be sure she had written them down correctly.

"Juan, I appreciate this more than you'll ever know, and I'll make it up to you. Now, one more favor. Please fax all of this information to Javier Valdez, Comandante of Guanajuato. She gave him all pertinent information in order for him to send the fax.

"I'll put a check in the mail to you today which should more than cover the telephone and fax expense."

"You don't need to do that," he said.

"Thank you, but I want to. Come and see us whenever you can. Thanks again."

After she hung up the receiver, she dialed Javier's private line. When he answered she told him he should have a fax coming in from her son-in-law in Texas, which she hoped he would read then put into his safe. "Also Javier, I need to talk to you in private. Can I come to your office as soon as you are free? This is very important."

"Of course. Can you be here in thirty minutes? I have an appointment, but I'll reschedule it."

"Thank you. I'll be there," she said, then replaced the receiver and ran downstairs to find Rick.

The three guys were watching television, munching potato chips and drinking cokes.

"Eating healthy, I see," she said. "Rick, I need to borrow you, and take you away from those chips before your cholesterol hits 300! Can you take me to town? I need to run an errand."

"Sure," he said, getting up.

"See you guys later," she said. "Jimmy, the roast is in the oven, and I'll be back in plenty of time to prepare the remainder of the dinner you requested."

When they got into the car, Rhonda told Rick all about her conversation with Juan.

"That's hard to believe," he said. "I'd like to be with you in your meeting with Javier."

She nodded, took a deep breathe and blew it out. He found a place to park and they went inside the ministerio publico, then were ushered into Javier's office.

"Has the fax come yet?" she asked.

"No, not yet."

"It should have been here by now," she complained. "Anyway, I have plenty to tell you, and it should come by the time I'm finished."

She began by telling him about hiring someone to tail

Ginger and that the calls had stopped. She reported that the broken window had been replaced and told about her close shave at the Pipila Monument and how somebody had pushed her, but Jimmy had caught her before she fell down the steps. "Whoever the "harasser" is, she is getting braver and more dangerous each day," she complained.

"I'm concerned about the incident at Pipila."

"So am I since I could have been killed!" Rhonda said visibly upset. "But you haven't heard anything yet. Listen to this." She took her notebook from her purse and began reading her notes to him. Just as she finished, the fax came.

He took the fax and read it, then sat there, shocked. "I'm stunned," he muttered. He continued to sit there his head in his hands, thinking for a couple of minutes, then he said, "Excuse me a minute," got up and told his secretary to send in two available officers.

When the men came into his office he gave them a piece of paper he had written on and said, "Pick her up and bring her in for questioning on charges of harassment. Tell her it has come to my attention that she has been harassing a family here in Guanajuato and I want to talk to her about it."

The men nodded and left.

The comandante turned to Rhonda and Rick and said, "You do understand that the person who is harassing you and the person who poisoned Ted may well be two separate people?"

"We realize that," said Rick. "We've discussed this thoroughly at home and have a notebook with motives and opportunity written by the name of each dinner guest. We amateur sleuths have also been engrossed in a secret investigation of our own."

"Rick, you don't need to tell everything you know," Rhonda scolded.

"I need to know everything you can tell me," Javier said.

"We've told you all the facts. The rest is gossip, hearsay, and supposition," Rhonda replied.

"Perhaps, I should hear that, too," he said.

"Some of it could be slander, so I'd prefer not to tell you unless it's absolutely necessary," she said.

Instead of replying, he sat lost in thought for a few moments.

"Perhaps we three should be like Hercule Poirot and employ the little grey cells," Rhonda suggested, grinning.

"Let's talk for a minute about each method of harassment," Javier said. The chocolates, sent without a card, may be considered a warning. They were not poisoned, but you were probably meant to think they were. The implication was that Ted's dessert was poisoned, therefore these chocolates, as your dessert, might also be poisoned. But why would anyone go to the trouble of buying and sending them to you, Rhonda?"

"We've talked about this at home, too, and the only reason we can think of is that Ginger was upset and wanted to vent her anger on Rhonda since she is Ted's heir," Rick replied.

"That's possible. Now, the second form of harassment was the phone calls, and that again could be the need to vent anger on Rhonda. Jealousy might be a second motive."

Rick nodded. "I think that's right. Probably repressed anger and the need to hurt that one who took something away from her also caused Ginger to throw the rock and break the window."

"That brings us to an actual attempt on Rhonda's life," said Javier, "but we have one big problem. We can't prove any of this. It's all supposition, all circumstantial."

"Funny how Ginger turned on me. She was friendly one day and my enemy the next. I've had people treat me this way before. People I had been very good to, and I still have no idea why they turned on me. No idea what I did to make them angry. I think I understand why Ginger is angry, though. I'd be upset too if Rick had died and had left a will naming another woman as his heir. But it's not my fault. I had no idea Ted had done that."

"Would you be willing to give Ginger whatever Ted left?" Rick asked.

"Before she began harassing me she could have had all except $2,000.00 which he owed me. But now I wouldn't give her a dime after all the trouble she has caused me."

"How much do you think he was worth?" Javier asked.

"If his estate was worth $2,000.00, I would be very surprised," Rhonda replied. "He even admitted there was no secret Swiss account. Surely Ginger is aware of that. That's why I can't believe her harassment is due to my being his heir. There's not enough money there to squabble over."

This case gets more intriguing every day, yet some of it simply doesn't make sense to me," the Comandante said, then added, "It's about time for Ginger to arrive, and I think I'll learn more if I question her alone. Do you mind?"

"Not at all," Rick replied. "We'll leave now."

"I'll phone you when I have some news. It might not be tonight. I expect her to be a tough nut to crack."

"I expect she's a nut in more ways than one," Rhonda quipped on her way out the door.

When they returned home Jimmy said, "Camila returned while you were gone, Mom, so Carlos has a report for you."

Rhonda smiled at Carlos, "Do we have a new suspect?" she asked.

"I don't think so. Camila said the professor's maid raved about what a wonderful man he is. She said she had worked for him for twenty years and there had never been a hint of scandal about him. She said women never spent the night in his home, that he was a religious man, an excellent father and grandfather. His family come for dinner every Sunday and often drop in through the week. She said he had many friends, he volunteers at the hospital, and that she couldn't say a bad word about him.

Camila said she asked if she could borrow some arsenic to kill some rats. The maid told her she didn't think there was any, but they would look for it. Camila said she helped the maid search for it, but they couldn't find any."

Then Camila told me that she saw Alejandra, the Lopez maid, as she was walking back to your house and Alejandra told her she had overheard Ted telling Ginger, the day before he died, that he wanted a divorce. "I want a quick Mexican divorce while we are here," he said.

"Ah ha! That's certainly a motive, isn't it?" said Rhonda who then went on into the kitchen and finished preparing dinner.

The roast had cooked slowly for several hours and it was tender and flavorful. The vegetables and the pie were not low in fat or cholesterol, but they tasted good.

"That dinner was sure delicious, Mom. Thanks," Jimmy said.

After dinner Rhonda asked Carlos if he would walk the dog with her. He agreed, and as they walked down the street she said, "I need to talk to you. It seems you and I have something in common. A packet of sugar has been planted in such a way as to incriminate both of us."

"What are you talking about?' he asked, puzzled.

"When I wash clothes I always check the pockets and remove any items left in them. I found a packet of sugar in the pocket of your black slacks before I washed them. It was the same type and brand that was planted in my desk by Ginger. The packet had been opened, then closed with a piece of tape.

I re-opened it and poured a little out in my hand and it was obvious that two white substances had been mixed together. One could have been arsenic. There were two substances mixed together in the packet that was hidden in my desk, also, and according to the lab report it was a mixture of sugar and arsenic."

"I have no idea how that packet got there. I didn't know it was in my pocket."

"Did you wear the pants anytime when you were around Ginger?"

"I wore them with a sports jacket the night we had dinner at the Lopez home, but I don't remember being close enough to Ginger that she could slip anything into my pocket."

"That's another mystery to be solved. Perhaps, she's like a pick pocket, except she slips items into pockets."

"Do you think she could have been in this house when nobody was home?" he asked.

"That's a scary thought. I don't know how she could get in. I did not have a key in my desk or anywhere in my office when she was here."

"To be on the safe side, perhaps we ought to change the locks," he said. "I will do it for you."

# Chapter Twenty-Six

The next day was Tuesday and Rhonda did not teach that day. She phoned Marta and told her that Jimmy had arrived safely.

"We want to meet him, Rhonda," she said.

"That's why I was calling you. Rick and Carlos told me that nobody will want to eat my cooking until the case is solved and until after I have been absolved as the 'mad poisoner', so I thought I would call Dominos to deliver pizza and invite you two for dinner so you can meet him. When are you available?"

"Is tonight too soon? It's our only free night this week."

"Tonight is fine, but I hate to take your only free night," said Rhonda.

"That's OK. We want to meet Jimmy, and both of us love pizza. Our favorite is Pepperoni. Hint! Hint!"

Rhonda laughed. "That's our favorite, too. See you about 7:00, if that's OK."

"We'll be there. Thanks for asking. But Rhonda, we're not afraid of your cooking. I'll eat anything you serve."

Camila arrived a few minutes later, and Rhonda thanked her for the detective work, as best as she could in her halting Spanish.

Rick and Rhonda were still taking a Spanish class from Dr. Carillo one night each week, and they were slowly progressing. However, since most of her friends spoke English, the conversation was always in English. She always spoke English with Carlos, too. It was just easier. She promised herself that when Ted's murder was solved, she would work harder at learning Spanish. She was taking a beginners class with Rick, which was a good review, but she should have been in an advanced class. She and Rick planned to take lessons the entire time they were in Mexico each year.

It was such a delight to be able to spend the winters in Guanajuato. The homes there had neither furnaces nor air conditioners. It had been about 65 to 75 degrees all winter. No snow, ice or mud. The tree in her courtyard was still green and the flowers were still blooming. She hoped she never had to spend another cold winter in Kansas. How she wished her mother was still alive and could have been here to spend these mild winters with them. She missed her so much.

Rhonda went upstairs to her office and began to write letters. She owed letters to her three aunts, and wanted to tell them the latest news about Ginger, and also about Nikki and Jimmy.

Carlos and Jimmy were sleepy heads, often not getting up before ten, so they fixed their own breakfast.

After she finished the letters she took Cleopatra for a walk, then went back upstairs to her office and wrote a chapter on the novel, Murder at the Post Office, which she had been working on for a couple of months. She only had about fifty more pages to write and it would be finished. Her next book would be titled Murder at the Church, the second book in her series of murder mysteries in Copeland, Arkansas. In her spare time, she still wrote two weekly newspaper food articles, for her column, the Reluctant Chef. And she was also contemplating writing a Three Ingredient- Vegetarian Cookbook since she had had many requests for one.

At one o'clock she served a simple luncheon of tuna salad sandwiches, green peas, ice cream, and fresh lemonade, since they would be eating fattening pepperoni pizza for dinner.

After lunch she phoned Nikki and told her how much she appreciated the information they had given her about Ginger and Ted.

"Guess what, Mom? We've learned something else that might interest you. You told Juan that Ted's second wife had been murdered and you wondered if Ted had killed her. Juan checked into that and learned that she had been killed during a robbery attempt at a store where she worked. The man who killed her was caught and sentenced to life imprisonment. Apparently, neither she nor Ted knew him."

"Ted talked like he didn't know who killed her."

"He probably didn't. The guy was only caught recently. He killed someone else and somehow they connected the two murders. He confessed that he had killed Marion Saxon also. I don't know the details. All I know is that they caught him, even though he had killed her several years ago."

"I'm glad to know Ted didn't do it," said Rhonda. "Tell Juan that I said to thank him. OK?"

"I will," she said.

"It's nice to know my former husband was not a murderer. I had worried about that."

"Mom, you've got to stop worrying about things you can't help. Remember what you always tell me. "You can't afford the luxury of a negative thought?"

Rhonda laughed, "I didn't know any of my advice ever sunk in. By the way, when are you and Juan coming to visit us? We miss you."

"We have been talking about coming, but we'd better wait until Carlos is gone. Where would we sleep?"

"You can have his room. He can sleep on the bed in my office. I'm sure he won't mind. Jimmy is sleeping on the Hide-a-bed sofa. He says it's more comfortable than his bed at the dorm. So come anytime. You haven't seen the house yet, and I know you will love it."

"We want to see Jimmy, too, and we've never met Carlos, so I'll talk to Juan tonight and let you know tomorrow night."

"I hope you'll come soon. Goodbye, darling. I love you."

"I love you, too, Mom. Bye."

Just as she began to write on her novel again, Javier phoned.

"Hi Rhonda. I just have about five minutes, but I told you I would call. We had some luck with Ginger, after she finally calmed down. She kept telling us how embarrassing it was to have two policemen drag her to the police station. Said she was so humiliated. She finally admitted sending you the candy and making the phone calls after we told her we had traced the calls and knew it was her. We took her fingerprints and told her they matched the ones on the candy box. We were lying, of course, but she didn't know it, so she confessed!"

Rhonda laughed, "Wow! Are you tricky! I'm impressed!"

"I got the idea after Agente Rivera told me about how tricky you are."

Rhonda giggled, "Did Ginger admit breaking my window and pushing me at the Pipila Monument?"

"No, she swears she didn't do either and that she was nowhere near Pipila, but she can't prove it because she said she was home alone, reading a book."

"So it's her word against Jimmy's and mine, though we can't prove it either. But who else could it have been? We'll have to think up a trick which will get her to confess."

"I tried to talk to her about her work and about her marriage to Ted, but she became hysterical, crying and saying, "I can't talk about Ted yet. I'm too sad about losing the love of my life." She broke down and cried so hard she couldn't answer any questions, so we gave up and took her home. I plan to bring her back in tomorrow for questioning."

"Didn't you know she was an actress in college? Had the main part in several plays? I guess I forgot to tell you that. She was probably faking that hysterical act so she wouldn't have to answer your questions."

"She won't get by with that next time. I'm glad you told me. Rhonda, put your 'thinking cap' on and help me think of a trick to use when she comes in, will you?"

"I will," she agreed, then asked, "what was her excuse for sending me the candy and harassing me on the phone?"

"She said she did it because she knew you had killed Ted. She said she saw you sprinkle arsenic over his dessert."

Rhonda burst out laughing. "The reason I think that is so funny is she phoned me last week and told me that Ted was blackmailing Dr. Gomez and she implied that the doctor had poisoned Ted's dessert during the diversion of the lost earring!"

"Why did she say Ted was blackmailing him?"

"I'd rather not say because I'm sure the story was merely a figment of her imagination. You'd think she could get sued for slander by telling such stories."

"Who knows it besides you?"

"I told Rick and Carlos. That's all, and they also think that she invented the story."

"Call me if you get an idea. I've got to run. Adiós!"

Since Ginger admitted making the phone calls, Rhonda asked Carlos to phone the night watchman and explain why they didn't need him anymore.

The pizza party was fun that evening. Rhonda and Rick were proud of Jimmy, who was so polite and friendly to their guests. The evening was informal and everyone seemed to enjoy themselves.

Before the evening was over, the conversation turned to Ted's murder.

"I heard who did it today," Rhonda said, tongue in cheek.

"Really?" Marta asked. "Who was it?"

"Javier told me that Ginger said I killed him!" she replied, an amused expression on her face.

They laughed. "Did she really?" asked Marta.

"Ginger said I sprinkled arsenic over his dessert when everyone was looking for your earring. She said she saw me do it! She seems to change her mind a lot. Last week she told me she saw a different person do it. Same scenario, however!"

Carlos said, "This all started when Anita insisted on having a farewell party for the Saxons. I don't know why she didn't just let them leave without any fanfare."

"How did you get involved in this, Carlos, since you live in Mexico City?" asked Francisco.

"Rhonda phoned me and told me that Anita had asked her to invite me. I planned to decline, until Rhonda said she had a bad feeling about this party. I've known her a long time and everytime she has a bad feeling something bad usually happens, so I decided she might need me and I'd better accept the invitation. So here I am! And I've imposed on Rhonda and Rick for nearly three weeks, but as a possible suspect I am not allowed to leave."

"Carlos is like one of the family," said Rick. "We're happy to have him."

Francisco said, "Rhonda, I'm intrigued about these feelings of yours. Give me an example, if you will."

"I kept trying to phone my mother one morning and she didn't answer, yet I knew she was home. I had a feeling that something was wrong, so I kept calling her every ten minutes for two hours. Finally I called my aunt who went to her house and broke a window to get in. They found her in bed. She had suffered a stroke, and even though they called an ambulance and got her to the hospital, she died six weeks later.

Another time, a year later, I had a feeling something was wrong with Granny. I kept calling her repeatedly and when she didn't answer, I phoned my uncle who told me that she was in the hospital having surgery for a broken hip at the very time I was calling her. She also died about six weeks later."

"That's spooky." Francisco said.

"I know it seems like a coincidence but it happens frequently. I tried to talk Anita out of having that farewell dinner, but she insisted on having it. Also, when Ted and Ginger first came to Guanajuato, I told Rick and Carlos I had a bad feeling about them coming here."

"See there, Francisco, there is such a thing as women's intuition," said Marta.

"I've always believed people should go with their feelings," he said, then added, "We must go. It's been a lovely evening and we really enjoyed meeting you, Jimmy."

Soon after they left, the phone rang and it was Juanita.

"Rhonda, could you come to my home for lunch tomorrow? I want to talk to you."

Knowing what she did about Juanita and Dr. Gomez and realizing that Juanita was a possible suspect in Ted's murder, she had no desire to eat anything that she cooked, so she thought quickly and said, "Juanita, thank you so much for inviting me, but I'm busy for lunch tomorrow. Would you like to come here about five tomorrow afternoon and we can talk privately?"

"I can tell you what I had to say over the phone. It's probably not significant, but I told Anita and she said I should tell you. The day before Ted died, he phoned me and wanted to talk about his salvation. We had a nice talk and I think I answered the questions he had. Then later that day I found a paper pushed under my front door. It was a poem he had written and ironically it was titled, "We All Walk Through Life in Peril." What do you make of that?"

"Juanita, I think he simply wanted to give you one of his poems as a thank you gift for taking time to talk to him."

"It was like he sensed that something was going to happen to him, and he wanted to get right with God before it was too late. We prayed together before he left."

"Thank you for sharing this with me, Juanita. I'm so glad you were there for him. Let's get together soon."

# Chapter Twenty-Seven

The three guys, Rick, Carlos, and Jimmy picked Rhonda up the next day after her class at the University and they went to the Castillo de Santa Cecilia for lunch and enjoyed a delicious buffet, then they returned home.

Jimmy soon talked his dad into taking him to the market, leaving Rhonda and Carlos at home.

"Carlos, I've got a lot to tell you about Ted and Ginger." Rhonda said. "I talked to Nikki and Juan and they finally got the information we had requested. Do you want to hear all of it?"

"Certainly," he said. "Shall we sit at the table in the breakfast nook and talk there?"

After they were settled, Rhonda took out her notes, consulted them and began. "Ted married a woman he knew from Kansas City then moved to Albuquerque about 1975 and was there until his wife was killed. The person who killed her has only recently been apprehended and prosecuted. He moved to San Antonio about 1990 where he worked at several different jobs in the past six years. In his spare time he wrote poetry and song lyrics, and it was true that he did sell several songs. He was talented and intelligent, but also had episodes of mental illness throughout his life, after about age 25. Two years ago he voluntarily committed himself to a mental institution and it was there that he met Ginger, but as a patient, not as a nurse."

"Oh? Is she schizophrenic, too?"

"Yes, apparently so. This is what Juan told me about her. She was born to wealthy parents. She was a straight A student, an artist and a talented actress. After graduating from college with a degree in nursing she got a job as a psychiatric nurse in a mental hospital. She worked there about two years, then she began having delusions and hallucinations, hearing voices telling her what to do, and her behavior became unpredictable, sometimes bizarre and frightening. For example, when she had an argument with another nurse, she grabbed a glass pitcher and broke it over her head. Since the woman required stitches, Ginger was fired."

"So, she was violent?" he asked.

"Yes, but at times she would withdraw from her family and friends, preferring to be alone. She wouldn't return phone calls and refused all invitations. Sometimes she heard voices telling her to harm others. Her mother called the police and had Ginger admitted to the hospital after she threatened her with a knife."

"How do you know all of these details?"

"The information came from her case study. This guy that Juan knows had access to it. Juan read the report to me and I took notes."

"Go ahead, Rhonda. This is somewhat surprising," he said. "She always acted normal to me."

"Apparently her illness caused impaired social functioning when she relapsed. She became suspicious of others and became more prone to violence as time went on. Stress from her job caused her symptoms to worsen, and she had problems concentrating. She lost two more jobs, and finally quit working altogether, then moved back home with her parents."

"Why did she lose her last two jobs?" Carlos inquired.

"As a psychiatric nurse Ginger had access to many medicines and she began taking drugs that were prescribed for her patients, then she would write on their charts that they had taken the medication. For example, she would write on a chart that she had given codeine for cough to a patient, then she took the drug herself. Finally, she was caught and fired.

Later she got a job working as a nurse for a psychiatrist. She had access to the doctor's prescription pads and knew how to write proper prescriptions, so she could get any drug she wanted. Also, the doctors have a lot of sample medications, which she would confiscate for herself. Her employer finally caught her and fired her.

After she moved home, she argued frequently with her parents and often hit her mother. One night she overheard her parents talking about disinheriting her and changing their will so that a favorite niece who had five children would inherit their home and much of their money.

"Were her parents going to provide for her in any way?" Carlos wanted to know.

"As her symptoms worsened, she caused them both so much stress and grief that they planned to tell her she had to move out, but they were going to set her up in a one bedroom townhouse which they owned and there would be a trust sufficient to pay for a car and all of her monthly expenses. Instead of being thankful that they were supplying her with a place to live, a car, food and for the necessities, she flew into a rage, grabbed her father's gun and shot them, killing them both.

She was brought to trial, but had been found not guilty due to insanity. In her case, I imagine the insanity defense was accurate. She was a dangerous psychotic killer who had murdered her own parents in order to inherit their home and fortune. She was sentenced to a mental hospital for life, but was released after twenty years."

"Was she in the same hospital that Ted was in?" Carlos asked.

"Yes, he had voluntarily committed himself because he realized he was relapsing. It was there that he met her and they became a steady couple. She told him that she would inherit her parents' home and wealth when she was released from the mental institution. She told him about the mansion, the Mercedes and the houseboat that she would own. Not to be outdone, he told her about the royalties from the songs he had written and about the million dollars he had stashed in a secret Swiss bank account.

She felt it was as easy to love a rich man as a poor one, and she pretended to have fallen in love with him. Soon he proposed and they planned to be married as soon as possible.

Eventually both were released from the hospital and they were married. To Ginger's chargrin, she learned that as the murderer of her parents, she could not inherit from them. By killing them, she did not even get the townhouse, a car or a trust fund.

She told Ted that while she was in the mental hospital, her parents had disinherited her and had given everything they owned to their church. Ted sympathized with her when she told him she had just learned they had both been killed in a car wreck.

Finally they both got jobs. Apparently there was a hospital desperate enough for a nurse that they didn't bother to check her references or past employment record. Ted also got a job in a publishing house. With steady money coming in, they rented a duplex and made a down payment on a car. They began attending church on a steady basis and seemed reasonably happy.

But before too long they began to have arguments about money. Ted didn't get home with much of his salary since he often played cards, gambled and lost much of his money. Soon the arguments were accompanied by mental and physical abuse. Ginger became tired of having to watch every word she said so that he wouldn't become angry. He was easily offended and fast to double up his fists and hit her when enraged.

Working as a nurse Ginger began her old habits of taking the patients' drugs after charting the medications on their charts to account for the medicine. However, she was soon caught and reprimanded, but when caught the second time she was fired. Some of Ted's symptoms began to return and he began having difficulties concentrating and focusing his attention on his tasks, which caused him to lose his job at the Publishing House. After laying around at their duplex for six weeks he finally took a job collecting tickets at a movie theater, a job which didn't require the concentration needed at his prior position. He eventually quit that job, also, which left them free to travel.

"Where did they get the money to travel?" Carlos wondered.

"Ginger had kept her address book during her many years of confinement in the institution, and when feeling up to it, she would write to her friends, giving the hospital as her address, but explaining that it was her place of employment.

When she and Ted were again without jobs she wrote to a former college roommate who lived in Guanajuato, Mexico, telling her that she and her husband planned to be in Mexico on vacation and that she would like to visit her. Ginger had enclosed her phone number, so Anita called her and invited her to stay with them when they were in Guanajuato. They came and they stayed, and stayed and stayed."

"I'll bet Anita is sorry she ever made that phone call," Carlos murmured.

"Isn't that the truth!" Rhonda exclaimed, then added, "that is the gist of Juan's report."

They were both silent for a few minutes, lost in their own thoughts. Finally Carlos asked, "Was there any mention of arsenic in the case study?"

"I can't believe I forgot to mention one of the most

important points. You know that as a nurse Ginger could get access to arsenic because it is an important treatment for certain skin diseases, anemia and also for some tropical parasitic diseases.

According to the report, Ginger at one time had a skin disease for which her doctor had prescribed arsenic. There's always the possibility that she still had some and that she brought it to Mexico with her," Rhonda concluded.

"But of course that would be very difficult to prove," Carlos muttered.

"Difficult, but not impossible," Rhonda said. "And an idea just popped into my head!"

# Chapter Twenty-Eight

Javier called Thursday morning and jokingly asked Rhonda if she was still "employing the little grey cells."

"Absolutely!" she responded, "and I have a plan. Carlos, Rick and I have discussed it and we think it might work. Do you have time to hear it?"

"Certainly."

She explained the plan, telling him it involved playing a trick on Ginger, then asked, "Shall we try it?"

"Why not?" he agreed. "What do we have to lose? She is supposed to be in my office this afternoon. Can you be here about four o'clock?"

"Sure."

"I hope this works," Javier said, "because at the present time I don't have enough evidence to convince a prosecutor to take any of the suspects to court. And until I do, I can't make an arrest."

"Perhaps you can make an arrest before this day is over."

"Rhonda, I'm sure you have an idea worth pursuing, but you must realize that Ginger might not be the "mad poisoner". It's possible that one of the other dinner guests had more of a motive than we are aware of. Ginger is innocent until proven guilty. See you at four."

Rick was sitting in the living room with Rhonda when Javier called, and they discussed her conversation with him. Rick offered to take her to the police station and stay with her during the confrontation with Ginger.

He added, "Do you remember that one of the policemen, when questioning us, mentioned something about hypnosis? As far as I know, the subject has not been brought up again."

"We certainly don't want to remind them of it either. I don't want to be hypnotized, do you?"

"No, I don't, but it's a tool which they might want to use on Ginger."

"That's an idea, Rick, but let's just wait and see what happens. Maybe it won't be necessary."

Changing the subject he asked, "Where are Carlos and Jimmy?"

"They went mountain climbing, which worries me. Maybe you ought to go and look for them?" She told him where they were, so Rick left to find them and bring them home.

While he was gone, Rhonda went to her office and began to make notes and write down a list of questions she planned to ask Ginger. She prepared for the meeting as she used to do when she was on a television cooking show in the States.

By the time she had finished her preparation and had practiced what she would say to Ginger in front of a mirror, Rick drove up with Carlos and Jimmy.

She ran downstairs to greet them. "I'm so thankful you all are OK. I was worried. It's dangerous to go mountain climbing."

"Ah Mom, you think everything is dangerous. I"m surprised you even let me walk down the street by myself to buy a package of potato chips."

Carlos and Rick chuckled. "You have to cut the apron strings, Rhonda," said Rick.

"Yes, Mom. I'm nineteen years old!"

"Jimmy, you're a baby. My baby," she grinned.

After a late lunch of what Carlos called American Tacos, served with fruit salad and her mother's Frosted Chocolate Sheet Cake, Rhonda showered, dressed and applied her make-up, then she and Rick were ready to leave for the police station.

Before leaving Rhonda asked Carlos if he wanted to go

along, but he replied he was too sore after climbing mountains.

"Jimmy and I will stay here and watch a movie, but I'll be anxious to hear all about it when you get home."

During the drive Rick and Rhonda prayed that God would give her the right words to say to Ginger.

When Rick and Rhonda were ushered into Javier's office, Ginger was already there and she looked angry. There were also two policeman standing against the wall.

"Hi Ginger. How are you?" Rhonda greeted her.

"OK," she replied, having the grace to look sheepish after all the things she had said about Rhonda behind her back.

Javier took over. "I want to thank each of you for coming here today. There are some things I'd like for us to discuss..."

Ginger interrupted, "I hope you've found out by now who killed my precious Ted. I miss him so much I can hardly bear it." Tears began to trickle down her cheeks. "I did everything to save him that was humanly possible, even gave him artificial respiration when I thought he was slipping away from me. And when I realized how ill he was, I insisted on taking him to the hospital. Ah, Senor," she said to Javier, becoming melodramatic and playing her part to the hilt, "you see before you a bereaved widow who has lost the love of her life! How can I live without him?"

Javier replied, "Senora, you have my most sincere sympathy, and I do want you to know we are doing everything we can to find out who poisoned him."

"Thank you so much, Senor Comandante," she replied, unsure of how to address him. She smiled at him, believing that he was impressed with her performance.

Javier then turned to Ginger and said, "Rhonda has something to tell you, now."

Rhonda looked directly into Ginger's eyes and said, "Ted came to my house two days before he was killed and told me that he thought you had been slowly trying to poison him. He said ..."

Ginger interrupted her. "You're crazy! I would never have harmed a hair on his head and he knew it! I loved him more than anything on earth. You are making up this story! It's quite obvious!"

Rhonda calmly said, "If you'll excuse me, I will continue with what I was saying. "Ted told me that if anything happened to him, he wanted me to go to the police and tell them that he thought you had poisoned him."

Ginger began to interrupt, but Rhonda held up her hand and said, "Let me continue. Ted also told me to tell the police that you have been diagnosed as paranoid schizophrenic, that you both had the same mental illness, and that he had met you when you were both patients in a mental hospital. He said..."

Ginger screamed, "That's a lie! I was a nurse when he met me. I was..."

Rhonda interrupted. "He said you had been a nurse on a psychiatric ward in a mental hospital at one time, but not when he met you. He also wanted me to tell the authorities that you had killed your parents and that you are prone to violence. He said he was afraid for his life..."

"You liar! Liar! Liar! Why would you say such things?" She screeched, then turned to Javier, "Make her shut up and get out of here! She killed Ted. I saw her poison him. I saw her sprinkle Arsenic on his dessert!"

"Ginger, why did you let him eat the dessert if you saw her poison it? Why didn't you knock the dessert off the table?" Javier asked.

"I...I... " she sputtered.

Before she could get one word out Rhonda continued, "Ted said you had been in the mental ward twenty years for murder one, that your attorney had used the insanity defense..."

She's lying," Ginger screamed, once again interrupting her. "I would never have hurt my parents."

"But Ted said you killed them, shot them both in cold blood because they threatened to disinherit you."

"That's a lie, and I can prove it because Ted didn't even know I had killed my parents. I told him they died in a car..." she paused, realizing what she had done, the mistake, she had just made.

Javier said, "Ginger, don't you think it's time you tell us the truth? We have your case history. We know all about your murder conviction, we know all about your confinement in the state mental hospital."

"But none of it is true. Rhonda caused me to get mixed up. She's been the cause of all of my troubles." Suddenly she jumped out of her chair, lunged for Rhonda, grabbed her hair and began to punch her in the face with her fists.

Rick was first to grab Ginger and pull her away from Rhonda then the two policemen were there dragging her away. Ginger was hysterical, screaming, "I hate her! I'll kill her, I'll kill her, I'll..."

One of the policemen stopped Ginger's tirade by slapping her face and commanding "Stop it right now! Shut up and I mean it!"

Ginger dissolved in a flood of tears, her shoulders shaking. When she finally calmed down Rhonda said, "Ted had recently told you he wanted a divorce. He was not the love of your life, you hated him. You were sick and tired of his abuse, but that's not why you killed him. You killed him for the money you thought he had stashed in Switzerland. Did you really believe that story? Didn't you realize that Ted was a liar and that he suffered from delusions of grandeur? Not only did Ted not have a cent in a Swiss bank, he never had a cent in any bank!"

"That's another of your lies!" Ginger screamed. "I have memorized his account number."

"The number he gave you was as fictitious as his Swiss account. It was part of his delusion."

"I don't believe you!" Ginger shouted, jumping up from her chair. The policeman now standing behind her shoved her back into her seat.

"Didn't you read the note Ted wrote to me which was attached to his will?" Rhonda asked.

"What note? I saw no note written to you."

Javier inquired, "You didn't read the note to 'Bubbles'?"

"Who's Bubbles?" she asked, glaring ominously at him.

"That was his nickname for me," Rhonda explained, "and he included with his will a letter to me which stated that 'the secret Swiss account was merely a figment of his imagination'!"

"This story is another one of your lies!" Ginger yelled at Rhonda.

"Calm down!" Javier ordered, then handed her a copy of the letter to Bubbles.

"Do you mean to tell me that you truly did not know about this letter?"

Ginger took the letter from him and read it, then re-read it. Some of the anger seemed to flow from her. Her shoulders slumped, she appeared to be defeated.

"You do recognize Ted's handwriting, don't you?" Javier asked.

Suddenly her shoulders stiffened and she again began to scream, "This is a trick! A dirty rotten lying trick! Someone forged this letter in a handwriting similar to Ted's just to trick me! I know there's a Swiss bank account. Ted gave me the combination and made me memorize it. He said the money would be mine if he died."

"He signed his death warrant when he told you that," said Javier. "You killed him because you wanted that money since you had not inherited your parent's wealth. You've killed twice for money, and ironically you didn't get any either time! Ted's death was for nothing since Rhonda was his heir."

"I'll contest his will!" she shouted.

Javier calmly asked, "Can his murderer inherit?"

Ginger jumped up from her chair, began screaming hysterically, then fell to the floor, pretending to faint.

"This is some more of her acting," said Rhonda. "Throw some water over her face."

Ginger then slowly appeared to come out of her faint, and said," Where am I?"

Rhonda said sternly, "Cut it out, Ginger. The game is up. We know all about your acting ability. We don't have time for your hysteria or your playacting. Get back in you seat where you belong!"

Surprisingly Ginger slowly got up and sat back down in her chair. She began to speak in a calm, clear voice, "Ted and I married each other for the money we thought the other had. Now, we find out that neither of us had a dime. The Bible says that the love of money is the root of all evil, and we have proved that to be true."

She slumped into her chair for a minute, her head toward her chest, then she straightened and said, "Ted and I were married a year and my life was in turmoil the entire time. Sure, I killed the creep, and he deserved it! I hated him, and yes, I poisoned him with arsenic. As a nurse, I knew he would die a slow, painful death--and I wanted him to suffer."

"Ginger, tell us what your life has been like since you came to Guanajuato," Javier said.

"Schizophrenia is not a sympathetic disease. Patients are made a figure of fun and ridicule, causing an inferiority complex. There are jokes and suspicion about one being in the bughouse or looney bin, and we are called a "nut", looney, crazy, batty, weird, etcetera.

Soon after we arrived in Guanajuato my symptoms began to return. In our rush to get to the airport on time I had forgotten to pack my medication and doctors' prescription pads. When I began to feel that I was on the verge of a relapse, I started taking Ted's pills, substituting his pills with a placebo, a pain killer that resembled his medication in size and color. When he began developing symptoms I told people he had probably forgotten to take his medicine, but in reality he was taking a placebo each day. I was basically allowing him to relapse while I took his pills and could continue to appear normal. I wanted him to relapse at first, so I could commit him to an institution and become his power of attorney. I thought I would then be able to get the money from his Swiss account.

However, Ted caught me exchanging his pills and he threatened to tell Felipe and Anita my secret. I did not want Anita to know that I was schizophrenic. She would have been afraid of me and would have insisted that we leave. So I decided to poison Ted to keep him quiet. He liked very sweet coffee, so I mixed arsenic with sugar in the sugar packets he had brought from the States. This slowly poisoned him, causing pigmentation on his skin accompanied by scaling hyperkeratosis on his palms and on the soles of his feet. He wanted to go to a dermatologist, but I told him it was caused by an allergy and that he would be fine as soon as we returned to the States. He also began to have transverse white lines on his fingernails, headaches, leg cramps, stinging and burning in his feet and he sometimes seemed to be quite confused. Besides these symptoms due to arsenical poisoning, he also began relapsing into schizophrenic again, becoming withdrawn and having delusions.

Actually, I did him a favor. He would never be completely well. I considered it a mercy killing. He couldn't keep a job, he gambled most of his money away, he was abusive, he would have spent much of his life in an institution, and may have eventually ended up as a homeless person living on the street. He's better off now. This was for the best."

Rhonda said, "There's one more question that needs to be answered, Ginger. You phoned me last week and told me that Ted went to Juanita's house and found her in bed with Dr. Gomez. Please set the record straight about that story."

Ginger looked down at the floor for a moment then raised her head and replied, "Ted did go to Juanita's home but Dr. Gomez was not there."

"Ted didn't ever find Juanita in bed with anyone, did he?"

"No."

"Thank you," said Rhonda. "I appreciate you telling me the truth about them."

Javier stood, "Ginger, I also want to thank you for your confession. I have to place you under arrest now, but you will be taken care of and given the medication you need."

He nodded to the two policemen, and one moved to each side of her, taking one of her arms, then they led her from the room.

When the door closed behind her, the three of them, Javier, Rick and Rhonda breathed a combined sigh of relief.

Javier asked, "Just for the record, Ted didn't really come to your house and tell you all these things, did he? You were so convincing, that you made me wonder."

"My lands, no! It was all lies!" she grinned. "It was a trick!"

"I can't believe it!" Javier exclaimed. "It worked! You did it!"

"We did it," Rhonda answered. "I couldn't have done it

without you, Rick and Carlos. This was a team effort."

Rick asked, "Are we allowed to call our friends and tell them that Ginger confessed? Some of them suspected Rhonda, I think, and I want them to know the truth."

"Go ahead. News of Ginger's arrest will be in the papers tomorrow."

"Thanks," said Rick, as he and Rhonda stood, preparing to leave.

Javier said, "I'm so thankful this is nearly over. I feel like shouting for joy!"

Rhonda grinned and said, "I feel like praying!" Then she closed her eyes, folded her hands and said, "Thank you, God!"

### American Tacos

| | |
|---|---|
| 1 lb ground sirloin | 3/4 cup water |
| 1 pkg dry taco seasoning mix | 1 can fat free refried |
| 1 dozen taco shells | beans |
| 8 chopped green onions | 1/2 cup sliced black |
| 1 cup shredded cheddar cheese | olives |
| 2 cups shredded lettuce | 1 cup thick and chunky |
| 1 chopped avocado | salsa |
| 1 chopped onion | 1 chopped tomato |

Fry meat and onion together and stir until brown and crumbled. Drain well. Stir in taco seasoning mix and water and cook as directed on package. Bake tortilla shells. Heat beans. Place beans, green onions, olives, cheese, lettuce, tomato, avocado and salsa in small individual bowls. Let each person fill taco shells, buffet style, with whatever he wants in his taco.

# Mother's Frosted Chocolate Cake

2 cups flour
2 cups sugar
1 stick butter
1/2 cup Crisco shortening
4 heaping Tbsp cocoa
1 or 2 tsp cinnamon

1 cup water
2 unbeaten eggs
1/2 cup buttermilk
1 tsp soda
1 tsp vanilla

Mix flour and sugar in large bowl and set aside. Boil together butter, Crisco, cocoa and water. Add to dry ingredients and immediately beat in eggs, buttermilk, cinnamon and soda. Bake in a 10x15" greased and floured sheet cake pan at 350 degrees for 20 minutes. Frost when cooled, but still warm.

Frosting:

1 stick butter
6 Tbsp buttermilk

4 Tbsp cocoa
1 box powdered sugar

Bring to a boil butter, buttermilk and cocoa. Remove from heat and stir in powdered sugar. Beat. Frost cake then sprinkle nuts over top.

The Dome of the Iglesia de la Companía de Jesús

# Chapter Twenty-Nine

On Sunday afternoon Rhonda, Rick and Jimmy went to the airport to pick up Nikki and Juan, who had come to visit them.

"We're so excited to see you!" gushed Rhonda, hugging them both. "What would we have done without you? If it hadn't been for the information you sent us, Ginger would still be running free!"

Rick and Jimmy took turns hugging them, too. "We're going to take you both out for the best dinner in town and entertain you royally," Rick said, hugging his daughter again.

"We'll take you up on that," said Juan. "We're hungry."

"Where's Carlos?" Nikki asked. "I've heard so much about him. I wanted to meet him."

"He volunteered to stay home and prepare sandwiches for us. We'll go home so you can unpack and eat a snack, then we'll show you the town of Guanajuato before dinner.

When they arrived home and Nikki and Juan were introduced to Carlos, he hugged them both, kissed Nikki's cheek and said, "You're as beautiful as your pictures."

Rhonda took them on a tour of the house and Nikki exclaimed, "I love the house, Mom."

That evening after a city tour and delicious dinner, Carlos said, "I'll be leaving tomorrow, but I want to invite all of you to come to Mexico City on Friday and stay at my home. I'll take you for a tour of the city, to the pyramids and to the Folklorico Ballet at the Palacio de Bellas Artes, then we'll go to Acapulco for a couple of days, and you'll all be my guests."

Everyone agreed they would really enjoy that.

The next morning there was an article in the newspaper

about Ted Saxon's murder being solved by Comandante Javier Valdez, who insisted credit should be given to Rick and Rhonda Winters, Carlos Selva and to Juan Preciosa whose information was invaluable during the investigation.

When Señora Winters, an author and English teacher at the University of Guanajuato, was asked why she became involved in the investigation she replied, "Not only was the murder committed at a dinner party at which I was present, but the arsenic was sprinkled over a dessert which I had prepared, making me a suspect."

Mrs. Winters became involved to clear her name and to help convict the murderer who had begun harassing and stalking her.

The article continued, giving detailed information concerning Senor Saxon's murder and his wife's confession and incarceration.

Not long after Rick and Rhonda returned home from taking Carlos to the bus station, the phone rang and it was Anne Hall, their friend from the States who had visited them when they were on their way to Mexico City. She said, "I'm calling to tell you that Derek and I won't be able to stop at Guanajuato to see you on our way home since we stayed too long in Acapulco, so we have to fly on home today."

"It would be nice to have seen you before you left, but we understand," said Rhonda. "You know you are always welcome to visit us. I hope you had a great vacation."

"We had a wonderful time," she said. "Do you know where Carlos is? We tried to call him last night when we arrived back in Mexico city, but he wasn't home."

"He's been here, but he's on his way back home right now. We've had excitement here in Guanajuato while you two lolled in the sun in Acapulco! Do you remember Ted from the Sunday School class?"

"Was he the one who talked too much?" she asked.

"That's the one!  His wife poisoned him with arsenic at a dinner party that we all attended, so Carlos, Rick and I have been playing 'Detective', and we helped solve the MURDER IN GUANAJUATO!"

Church of San Diego and Pípila statue
perched on mountaintop

# Chapter Thirty

Eventually Ginger was taken to court and tried for first degree murder. She was found not guilty by reason of insanity in the charge of murdering her husband on March 25, 1998 and was sentenced to a maximum security mental hospital for life, being both a danger to herself and to others.

After she was sentenced, she turned to Rhonda and said menacingly, "Someday I'll get out for good behavior and I'll come after you with Ted's .357 Magnum."

Rhonda replied, "¡Qué será, será!" What will be, will be!

The End!

# Index of Recipes

**ORDER BLANK**

NAME _____

ADDRESS _____

CITY & STATE _____ ZIP _____

How many copies? _____ Amount enclosed _____
       Price per book ................................... $8.95
       Postage & handling ........................... 1.55
       Total ............................................... $10.50
Please make checks payable to:
                  Ruthie Wornall
Mail orders to:          Ruthie Wornall
                  9800 W. 104th St.
                  Overland, KS 66212

------------------------------------------------

**ORDER BLANK**

NAME _____

ADDRESS _____

CITY & STATE _____ ZIP _____

How many copies? _____ Amount enclosed _____
       Price per book ................................... $8.95
       Postage & handling ........................... 1.55
       Total ............................................... $10.50
Please make checks payable to:
                  Ruthie Wornall
Mail orders to:          Ruthie Wornall
                  9800 W. 104th St.
                  Overland, KS 66212